THE CAVES

Norman Thaddeus Vane
and R. Rude

MAJOR BOOKS • CANOGA PARK, CALIFORNIA

This novel was co-written, but is based on the original story by Norman Thaddeus Vane, who created the original idea and all the characters and dialogue.

Copyright © 1977 by Norman Thaddeus Vane
All rights reserved

MAJOR BOOKS
21335 Roscoe Boulevard
Canoga Park, California 91304

First printing .... *June, 1977*
Second printing .... *May, 1979*

Printed in the United States of America

ISBN 0-89041-243-X

THE CAVES

This story is based on a little known, but authentic, historical fact. However, the authors wish to make it quite clear that this is in its entirety a work of fiction. To this day, the Caves in the Huachuca Mountains in southern Arizona near the Mexican border do exist. Geronimo once sought refuge in them. To this day, the way out of the Caves remains an Apache secret.

Chapter One

The stark southern Arizona Huachuca Mountain Range jaggedly swept up the bleak and desolate prairie. To the west was the Sonora Desert, a land of three-pronged cacti and little else. To the east, more mountains of parched, sun-bleached rocks, all lit by the sun's blood-red glow.

To this arid plain of dried water holes and flaking white skulls came a far-off sound. At first it was dispelled, by the air currents on which vultures floated. But the desert voice was insistent, breaking through the wind with its angry beat. The noise stopped abruptly, a moment's silence, and then it came again—from another direction. The two mountain ranges were speaking—but from where, from whom?

There was no sign of breathing life, except high in the skies. A finger of smoke, curling skyward answered the drums. Rapid puffs, then a long, broad cloud swirled up into the breezes and dissipated. The deadly pall that hung over the desert was broken. But nowhere was there a sign of human life.

The wind swept down over the calcified plain. Whirling funnels of dust were twisted up above the land. Suddenly, low on the horizon four black specks appeared, moving through the undulating, shimmering waves of heat. The cloud of yellow dust built as the specks grew larger. The sound of the drums picked up a staccato beat, as hoofbeats broke into the tempo. Ponies, some with riders, some without, moved across the arid, cracked land. A caravan of dirt-caked, sweat-soaked beasts racing from one range to the other.

There were four riders, two riding bareback. They

9

beat their half-dead animals on. Behind the riders were five horses, tied and trailing. The ponies' pained neighs and exhausted squeals echoed across the once-quiet wasteland. Arms struck across the horses' matted rumps. Their nostrils flared. Blood trickled down to their frothing mouths, leaving their open lips tinged with pink foam. One of the horses being led stumbled, its jerking fall almost pulling the last rider out of his saddle. Hardly slowing down, he dragged the failing animal up. The horses' eyes flashed wild, white, and frightened. Seared hands held the rawhide reins and ropes.

The riders' hands were leathered, their skin red, their clothes a mixture of White and Indian. Tattered skin leggings were drenched in sweat—theirs and the animals'. One Indian on a heaving pinto wore his leggings tightly laced over ballooning green pants. His shoes were cracked and torn, their beige tops smeared and stained with human blood. The others were wrapped in dark-stained clothes, which were tightly tied around their arms and waists over military coats. Their uniforms could have been traded years ago before the wars, but more likely than not they were taken off the dead. They were running through their own lands like a pack of hunted dogs.

The front rider's face was almost hidden by the wet band tied low around his forehead. Black, wet hair fell from underneath a high, crumpled hat. He wore the mask of the land. The years of fighting the mountains and desert had given him a hunted look. But deeper lines were etched and slashed across his face. Angry, twisted, bitter lines.

One by one the horses slowed on a small rise in the flat expanse. Heads lowered, sweat running down their long, thin foreheads, the horses gulped for air. Their sides heaved. They coughed as they breathed in dust. The four Apache riders quickly dismounted and leaned heavily against the animals. Their legs buckled slightly from muscles that had been tightly clenched. The three younger braves looked to the leader. They watched as he led his panting horse to the base of a telegraph pole. He signaled to the youngest, Taza.

A message was being tapped out on the telegraph lines over their heads. In a small broken shack in the compound of Fort Huachuca, a husky, parched voice paused impatiently for the operator.

> ". . . on the 19th of May, 1884, a party of forty Chiricahua Apache prisoners, headed by Geronimo, escaped from the White Mountain Reserve in Arizona and resumed their raids. . . ."

Taza began to grope through the rows of leather, bullet-strung belts, which criss-crossed his chest and back. He quickly unbuckled the holsters from his hips, letting two Colt .45's drop at his feet. The others watched as he stripped out of his explosive casing. The leader nervously scanned the horizon, watching for any movement.

> ". . . on May 25th, the Fourth Cavalry led by Major Emmet Pilcher out of Fort Huachuca engaged the band thirty-nine miles northwest of the Mexican border. . . ."

Leading his horse to the pole, Taza swung up on him lightly. The horse fidgeted, throwing his head, but did not move. Taza steadied himself on the animal's scrubby back. He began to climb the pole. The rough, splintered wood dug into his skin. He shimmied up suffering the wood slivers with soft Apache curses.

> ". . . following the trail of mounting dead, past burned-out farms and mine stakes. The cavalry picked up under its protection many lost civilians. The chief object of the

troops will be to capture or destroy the
band of hostile Apache Indians. Stop."

Almost immediately the wires began clicking their
reply.

"Government offers rewards in gold for
Apache scalps—one hundred dollars for
one warrior's scalp, fifty for one squaw,
twenty-five for an Indian child. As per
orders from Congress, use any means nec-
essary to kill all grown Apaches. Allow no
Indian to escape alive. Signed, General
George Crook. Repeat. Kill all. . . ."

The wires abruptly sparked and fell to the ground.
Clinging precariously to the top of the pole, Taza
slashed his knife once more. A boyish grin crossed
his face. He knew that the White Man depended too
much on these thin wires, which were so easily cut. He
shimmied two-thirds of the way down and nimbly
leapt to the ground.

The leader's eyes caught movement on the horizon.
A cloud of sand rose in the distant heat waves. He
stared briefly through the haze as the dust sharpened
into form. Then, quickly, without a word, he swung up
on his horse. The others without hesitation mounted
and followed, leaving only the dangling wires as mute
evidence.

The Apaches were soon lost in the maze of gullies and
cracked ravines. They moved swiftly and left behind
little dust. Their ponies' hooves, shoeless and wrapped
in rawhide boots, thudded softly onto bedrock. The
wind had swept away the thin layer of earth from the
granite floors of the mountains. The hills were barren,
infertile stone wastelands of little use to anyone. But to
the Apache, they were sacred, having given breath to
the serpent, the bird, and the beast. From these mountains came the Mother of Life, White Painted Woman,

and her offspring, Child of the Water, from whom all Apaches were born. Into the hills now fled her children, led by the weary and reluctant warrior, son of no chief, leader of his beleaguered few, Geronimo.

As the Indian ponies had moved across the arid plains, a larger group now raced through the heat and dust. Two horses ranged ahead of the main group, which spread out in a limping line nearly a mile long. The lead rider on a sleek gray horse spurred the animal up the sharp rise to the telegraph poles. He angrily jerked the horse to a stop, whirling around in his saddle and yelling to the other rider a few dozen feet behind.

"Dammit, Sergeant! What's Bernard doing back there with those civilians? We've lost a good six hours!" Major Emmett Pilcher, United States Fourth Cavalry, slid down from his horse. He was in his early forties, with a face of clay, as craggy as the bitter land on which he stood. His coarse, rough voice suited the rest of him. His uniform was crusted in grime and soaked through with sweat. His unshaven face abruptly turned from the sergeant to the hanging telegraph wires. He slapped his thigh with the long reins in his hand. His horse's head jolted away from him, staring at him warily, as if waiting to be struck.

The major's face was a map of crosscurrents—Scots, Irish, English—tempered badly like impure iron—with the ore of German and Scandinavian blood. The combination seethed, rather than settled in his veins—making him a curiosity of nature—somewhere between a distempered prairie wolf and a bulldog. His Scots' ancestry gave him a rawboned solidity; his Irish and English blood bristled hostility in every instinct. Reflected in his blue-green eyes was his journeyman's soul. The jaw was too thick, but the lips too full to be a man's man. His big-boned hands and feet were his German curse. His head was topped by a bristle and thistle of carrot-blonde-gray streaked stands of mismatched hair, which compared unfavorably to his horse's. He had an image of himself and so did his men. They quivered before him—and his changing moods—his feigned temper, which was mostly display. . . .

Sergeant Talbot rode back to the main group, down past the straggling line of riders—about half dressed in blue, gold-striped uniforms of the cavalry, the rest civilians, men and women, homeless and exhausted. Through narrowed eyes, he shot arrows of contempt at them. They spread before him like circles on a pond from an angry stone. The sergeant hailed from Pennsylvania, but that was long ago in another world and he hardly remembered the boy he was. His shanks of muscle slithered under his shirt threateningly, his gnarled, knotted, calloused fingers aiming the animal, slipshod among them. If the major was the devil, Sergeant Talbot was his advocate. Often a sharp slash of whip across a man's or animal's ass made his point.

Private Orley quickly joined the major on the top of the rise. He was a boy—a twenty-year-old boy—and always would be. A string of lean meat that ended in a baby face—where two beacons of eyes, blushed in outward innocence. He was from the South, even without opening his mouth, his slink swore it. He was a bumpkin overwhelmed by eagerness. He climbed like a creature of the woods after possum or squirrel—or sometimes eggs—a hundred feet straight up a pine, and he plucked without so much as a thank-ye-kindly from a nest, unmindful of the blatant cries of the mother hawk. Yes, Orley was the camp fool and the cavalry bobcat. Up, up he would slither—teeth gritted—eyes on his objective.

Private Orley deftly tied a rope around his waist and began climbing to the top of the telegraph pole. Dangling from his one leather-gloved hand were the wires—their only connection with the outside world. He expertly spliced the severed lines. The task finished, he rested at the top of the pole. "They're joined, Major!" Orley called down. He leaned his chin against the pole, waiting for his breath to catch up with him.

14

"Goddamn, shimmy on down!" the major's voice cracked. Orley immediately lunged down the pole, picking up a handful of splinters at every move. His ungloved hand was raw and bleeding. He walked over to several other, dirt-caked, sweating troopers who were watching over a cluster of soaken wet horses. "Damn splinters like to tore my skin right off!" Orley limped off, beating the dust out of his uniform with his cap.

Major Pilcher paced nervously under the pole. At his side, squatting on the ground in front of a keyboard and an old battery was Joshua Barrett. His woven suit with vest and bow tie was torn and frayed. Despite the thick coat of dirt covering him from head to foot, he still carried an air. A gnawed pencil stuck out of his jacket pocket. On the ground beside him were several tattered notebooks and a dented felt hat. Barrett looked up at the major, fingers poised on the keyboard.

To Barrett, the major was a crude nugget. He saw him as a gruff pro with still-to-be-fathomed motives, a disciplined and conditioned mind, not too bright, but cunning—but then, Barrett viewed him from an intellectual's perch. The major surmised Barrett simply as a thorn imposed in his side, stuck there by the government like an unwanted regulation. He knew he was shabby in contrast to the reporter's mentality—him and his letters with seals and stamps stating this and that, thus and so. Him with his college manners and words. His presence made the major swallow and curb his tongue. Barrett stuck out in the group like a sore, educated thumb. He even looked like a thumb. With his bright, piercing eyes—damn him!—intelligent eyes—and an always questioning mouth, out of which the words tumbled, with a faint ring of contempt. He'd teach him country manners before the trip was out.

Barrett felt the major's observations painfully. He knew he was a sore thumb to him. This job was a reward—an accolade for fifteen years of Washington columns—long-winded and much quoted—awards

15

from his own press and pats on the back from senators. His editorials, like Horace Greeley's, had often touched a nation's heart. During the Civil War, he was at the front. Then when Lincoln was assassinated, it was Barrett who had dipped his pen in blood and poured out a nation's grief in an eloquence profound. And now, he was assigned to cover another death—an Indian nation's—symbolized by one last warrior. For this he had come west—months of trains and small hotels, three forts—and finally, he was riding the wind with the Fourth Cavalry in pursuit of what—?

The major continued pacing, waiting for the words to come to him. Words were not his game. They were Barrett's. His taste was in the hunt, the chase, the fight. He cleared his throat, trying vainly to dislodge several weeks of dust from his mouth.

"Tell the colonel," he paused, as Barrett slowly tapped out the message, "the original Apache party's been wiped out by half."

Barrett quickly transferred this to dots and dashes. He stopped, with an edge in his voice, mixed with distaste for the unorthodox major, "Should I tell the colonel about our losses?"

"Just say," he hesitated, "we lost over twenty soldiers. But picked up nine civvies along the way. They're all under our care and protection now, includin' two women." The major stopped to let Barrett catch up with him. His face twisted with impatience as he watched him fumble with the keys. He would be glad to unload the unwanted reporter with the liberal eastern views. The sooner the better, as far as he was concerned. Barrett's soft-minded philosophizing had no place in this barren, desolate land. Already there was the beginning of a great hostility between the two men—a conflict of cultures, brought together by accident and uneasily pitted and committed to the same destiny with different methods.

"Let's see, what else?" The major broke off from Barrett's gaze. He continued to pace, a bemused grin

16

on his face as Barrett awkwardly resumed the tapping. "Just say the raiding party broke up into small groups to facilitate escape. We are chasing four of them into the Huachuca Mountains. The splinter party before us I believe to be Geronimo himself." Then he added, "That should make the bastards sit up!" Barrett started to transfer this into code. "Don't tap that. Where's your sense?"

"Anything else?"

The major lit up a cheroot and puffed on it expansively. "Tell them I left thirteen troopers on guard back at the fort—under the command of Captain Arapahoe Brown. Stop."

Barrett's finger vibrated the keys loudly, then stopped, having caught up. "Yes?"

"Our position is just above the Mexican border. Five miles south of the Nogales-Bisbee turnoff. Stop. Then sign it, Emmett Pilcher, Major U.S. Fourth Cavalry."

·The major swung up onto his horse, collecting the reins of the high-spirited animal. He touched the horse's neck fondly, easing him around to face the mountains. Somewhere off in those hills was Geronimo.

"Major, sir—"

"Yes, Mr. Barrett?"

"Can I take ten minutes to telegraph my paper in St. Louis?"

"I said we was only stoppin' long enough to fix this wire and get a message back to headquarters, didn't I?"

"Yes, Major. But—it's been over a week since my paper heard from me. This is the last of the telegraph wire. I won't get another chance to—"

Turning on his nervous horse, the major snapped, "Your story is ridin' up ahead, Mr. Barrett. Pack up that box and batteries, we're movin' out!"

The major and the sergeant were both helplessly annoyed by the yoke of stragglers clutching around their necks. They could not leave them behind, that would be death for sure. Sergeant Talbot rode his horse past the weary troopers.

"Mount up, boys. No time for sleeping. Corporal Goddin! On the double!" He came up to Lieutenant Wesley Bernard and reined his horse up next to him. "The major wants you up ahead, Lieutenant."

Despite his dirt and weariness, the lieutenant's West Point background was still obvious. He had missed the Great War by a few years and felt cheated. His zeal for manhood overshadowed his soft, quiet exterior. But under that was a desperate, trapped, insecure civilian. The lieutenant had only been in uniform four years—the civilian had been playing the role for eighteen. The lieutenant had a face for the world to see—the boy from Bethesda, Maryland, had a mask. It always smiled, it was his stamp. Put there by an overpowering mother—and only the memory of a dead father and five sisters and three aunts.

He had been raised by women and hid behind skirts till he was nine. His first toy had been a doll—when he was eleven he shot it dead. His second toy had been a horse—it was the beginning of his long escape—his flight, first to fancy, then to an unprepared and ill-equipped reality: a military school in Virginia, later the Point.

But still his women haunted him—their voices—feminine and shrill, commanding him in his dreams to fetch and jump. They wrote him long letters—*all* of them (*each* of which he was under obligation to reply to) and knitted objects for him—gloves—*gloves* in Arizona! Non-regulation to boot. And prayed for him! If the prayers of nine women could keep one man in safety, Wesley Bernard was safe, safe as in his mother's womb. . . .

The lieutenant eagerly spurred his horse forward and galloped past the slow-moving entourage. "You people are gonna keep up or you'll answer to me. Understood?" He did not wait for any answers, but rode down to the end of the line and swatted an overloaded mule with his reins. "Move this thing, old-timer, or shoot it!"

Venable Brown glowered at him through a wiry mass of hair, which sprouted from his head and face. He was a lead nugget who had spent a lifetime in the fantasy of chasing fool's gold. In his own words, he had found the pot at the end of the rainbow "was a pissin' pot." There was no gold and *he* was the fool. He had come west as a young man in '48. He found and lost a lode at Sutters— panned and scraped the swirling waters of his youth, his manhood, two wives, a dozen claims, and a hundred mules, to no avail. Not even dust clung to his stubby fingers, but the dream still danced in his tortured brain. He would strike pay dirt again. The whole shebang would be his "as far as the eye can see." If he did not find that mine, he would only settle for a tombstone. The old man said nothing, just spat a black mouthful of tobacco juice at the officer's foot and lugged his pack animal on. . . .

High on a rocky cliff, beyond the sight and hearing of the cavalry, the drums began to roll again. A few vultures scattered at the sound. Their heavy wings lifted them up and away from the oozing carcass of a fallen antelope. A bunch of scavenging javelinas froze in their tracks. Then, grunting and squealing, they scat- tered among the rocks. One animal, however, looked toward the drums, not in fear. It listened attentively, then slowly raised its head and howled. The wolf listened again, then turned back to watch the ap- proaching cloud churned up by the cavalry. Suddenly, the wolf began to shed his skin. He rose off his hands and knees, revealing a two-legged animal, un- mistakably Indian. His black eyes followed the cavalry.

Chapter Two

The level terrain was beginning to break up. The ravines, gutted by flash floods in the winter, were now cracked and dangerous. The Apaches plunged down into a deep gully. Their horses' hooves sent huge clumps of clay tumbling to the bottom. They were close to the hills, having left the baking plain behind. A coolness and a smell of water teased the air. The horses' nostrils flared; they pricked up their ears and moved faster. They carefully picked their way into the mouth of a tremendous canyon. The sharp cliffs zigzagged in such a way that the entrance was hidden from fifty yards off.

The walls of the canyon rose over eight thousand feet. Inside it were miles of cliffs, angles of sharp, unclimbable granite, which towered and leaned over parched, dry, caked ground. In the hot, searing sky were slowly circling condors. A few perched patiently on the limbs of sun-wilted trees. The birds were ominous. They waited for the flesh of the dead or the soon to be. . . .

Geronimo waved his hand briefly. Taza leaned his head wearily on his pony's neck and tried to gain his breath. White Horse, his face smeared with war paint, his hair tied with a thin piece of rawhide, quickly jumped off his mount. His pony was limping badly. White Horse tenderly felt its puffing, blood-covered fetlock. He looked over to Geronimo to see if there was time. The old warrior simply nodded, then returned his gaze to the mouth of the canyon. White Horse brought up one of the other ponies. He quickly unsaddled the lame mount, loading it with the pack of food that had been on the other horse. Saddling the fresher mount, he swung up, his eyes riveted on their leader.

Naiche, his green pants flapping in the breeze, turned his horse to Geronimo. He was old for forty. His face wore the marks of many wars. His eyes were brimmed with a blind revenge. Naiche was quick to kill. He knew no other way. Geronimo, in his fifty-five years, had learned to temper his vengeance with cunning. Two obsidian beads were in the center of his eyes. A thin slash of perpetually pursed and never-smiling lips crossed his mouth. His dignity was not inbred, but it was there in his every move, forged by suffering and sorrow in the heat of countless battles, in the winter of his life.

Geronimo moved his horse back to the lip of the canyon. Far off on the plain was the rising smoke and yellow dust of many horses. His gnarled hand shielded his narrowed eyes from the sun. He studied the dust intently, then jerked his horse nervously, edging it back to the others and pointed farther into the canyon. Silently with no protests they followed him deeper into the dead-end canyon. They broke into a gallop and raced straight toward the center of the gorge.

The major pulled up his horse at the edge of a wide arroyo. He stared angrily into the face of the impenetrable mountains. Sheer walls confronted him with no distinguishable breaks. The black granite blended in with the dark shadows into one massive sheet.

Lieutenant Bernard was breathing as heavily as his horse. Behind him trailed the troopers. They were a motley group, half-baked and abused. A couple were recent immigrants, transplanted bodies taking hold in the dry, baked clay of the West. They had fled conscription in Europe to wind up in the U.S. Army, when broke and hungry in the wild, new land. Some were in purely for the free hike west to silver and gold. Others were hard ones—tough nuts—bums, who had been given a choice of jail or duty. Boys from the midlands who had chosen this to the bleak life of the farms or the debts and grime of city slums. Indian fighting was something out of dime novels and wild west shows, melodramas they were soon acting out themselves and the bullets were all too real.

And no place to desert. Too easy to be shot and no-where to go. They were stuck with at least five years of military service. They were regular army, shuffled from Fort Riley in Kansas, to Fort Gibson to Fort Huachuca. They had learned to fight in battle and despite all their whining and complaining, they were beaten, literally, into tough soldiers. The first year had broken them, the second had prepared them, and by the third, their trial by fire had forged them.

Suddenly, from behind some rocks, a filthy, swaggering Indian appeared. The half-breed scout, Dull Knife, motioned to the major. The two men gesticulated rapidly in Apache.

Dull Knife spoke a dozen Indian tongues; he had been kicked around on as many reservations. He was a half-breed, raised by soldiers, acquiring all their bad habits, but still instilled with his boyhood instincts, his Indian nature. His cunning was as sharp as a weasel's. He could shoot, but he would not fight against an Indian. He bird-dogged the cavalry, but never raised a hand to a brother. He was in between the two races and despised by both. At age nineteen, he cut off a squaw's nose and was jailed. At twenty-two, he sold illegal tiswin and was caught three times. He stole ponies, then cattle. He became a scavenger, a renegade, a two-legged animal. Jailed a dozen times, he never learned. Finally, befriended by the major, he had been released—as a scout. At last, he had found a niche. He was fed, clothed, and paid in gold coin. He had value. But one day Dull Knife knew in his heart he would pay the price of being the outcast. Till then, he was given tiswin to block out his fear and guilt. He was a man without people, a loner.

Then, as abruptly as he had appeared, Dull Knife again vanished into the rocks. The major spurred his horse after him.

The troopers' horses raced between, under, and through sharp, dead branches, which tore at their uniforms and faces. Heavy, spined mulberry bushes jabbed into their skin ripping it. They careened along a narrowing trail around a tight corner to a stop. They had reached the tongue of the canyon. Far inside, at least two miles ahead, a faint, dusty cloud could be seen.

Lieutenant Bernard inched his horse forward. He strained to take in the wide expanse of the mammoth gorge. Almost fearfully, he asked, "Where are they heading, sir?"

"Beats the shit outta me. But, there's *no* way outta this canyon!"

"They ain't goin' up the canyon walls," the sergeant added.

The major nodded, "We got them cut off, long as we hold the mouth!"

"They gotta come back to us, Major!" the sergeant whooped.

The lieutenant turned to the major apprehensively, "I don't get it—what are they up to?"

"They're not up to nothing, son. They thought they could lose us, but they foxed themselves right into our hands."

"Major, I never seen this canyon before, have you?" the sergeant asked, his eyes scanning the depths of stone.

"It's not on the map, Sergeant. But if it's the one I think it is, I heard of it all right."

"What's it called?" Lieutenant Bernard asked, as he continued to gaze into the deep walls of shadows.

"Skeleton Canyon."

"I thought that was just an old Indian tale."

"So did I, Sergeant!"

"Is it Geronimo?"

"Follow me, Lieutenant—you can damn well ask him yourself!" The major urged his horse forward. The animal slid on its haunches down a loose gravel embankment to the floor of the canyon. Bernard and Talbot were on his heels, followed by the rest. The horses galloped lightly, as if refreshed by the knowledge that their hard ride would soon be over. The major pushed the horse faster and harder as the gap between his old foe diminished. His back strained eagerly as he approached the center of the canyon.

He could see them clearly now, could see the Apaches whipping their horses. They were galloping straight into the canyon walls. It was as if they were inviting death, rather than capture. The major briefly turned his head, waving his Winchester. When he turned back—they had disappeared. His horse slid to a stop, scraping its haunches on the coarse ground. He scanned the area looking for any signs of the renegades.

After a few long moments of looking around in disbelief and wonder, the major hissed, "They're *gone!*" Then, he yelled back at the slowing troops, "Dammit, they're gone!"

"Gone where?" the lieutenant anxiously peered into the walls around them. "You think they circled back, sir?"

"Circled back *where,* Lieutenant?" the major shouted. "You tell me how in hell they passed us without us seein' them!"

The sergeant shook his head. "Gawd! I just looked away two shakes of muh horse's tail and when I looked back—"

"They was air . . ." the major sighed, still unable to recover from the unexpected turn of events.

"That looks like solid rock to me, Major," Talbot added, drawing in his breath in a low whistle.

The major's eyes burned into the solid stone at the base of the mountain. "Goddamn, I can't believe it. Just when we had them trapped—they rode into rock. Four Indians and nine ponies *disappeared!*"

All three stared straight into the endless, rising, jagged, impenetrable rock walls of the canyon. There was nothing but miles and miles of granite.

Chapter
Three

A cool mist rose in heavy vaporous clouds. The only sounds were the rhythmic dripping of water and a strange muffled high-pitched chirping that bounced back and forth between the slick, wet walls. They glistened with a strange phosphorescent moss. A putrid smell of rotted stone and decomposed matter permeated the air.

The quiet, padded footsteps of horses drifted through the mists. Suddenly, the chirping swelled in alarm. A giant rush of bats' wings and bodies thudded against the stone. Then slowly subsided as the sound was carried off into the dark distance. By the side of the steaming, rocky pool, Geronimo paused to drink. The others dropped to their knees at his side. Taza plunged his head and shoulders under the water. White Horse drank quickly, then he filled a rawhide pouch with green water and went to his lame pony. He gently let the water run over the infected fetlock. Then, he softly dabbed the fleshy gap clean. Taza led the other animals to the pool. The horses splashed and snorted in the water, blowing the thick grit out of their nostrils. Naiche, rifle in hand, cautiously retraced their steps a dozen yards and peered into the dark. His ears, as keen as the bats', listened. Satisfied that they had not been followed, he returned to the group and hunched down and waited.

Geronimo studied the towering walls around him. A peaceful, reverent look replaced the weariness in his face. High above him in the rocky ceiling were narrow crevices which let in broken streaks of shimmering sunlight. The eerie light revealed a whole panorama and network of twisted caves and caverns. A maze of tunnels led off in every direction from the vast room in which they had paused.

He motioned to the others. It was time to move again. They rode past several tunnels and into an underground stone passageway. It was a seemingly endless, intricate, and complex beehive in an underground world. The war party, now refreshed, moved purposefully past walls, rock shelves, and ledges, on which were clustered thousands of staring, hanging bats. On and on they went making their way almost leisurely now over treacherous, slippery rock formations, past dense, dripping catacombs. Huge monuments spanned over and around them. Time-shaped statues of limestone dripped from the ceilings. Stalagmites and stalactites formed gigantic pillars in their subterranean palace.

Their religion told them that White Painted Woman had raised her offspring, Child of the Water, in a cave. The caverns had brought life to their race. Now, they were giving life to her sons. The Apaches moved quietly, only their ponies' hooves resounded on the rock. Their legends were filled with stories of the Caves. The long, twisting journey through the darkened grotto was a brief flight into the land of the spirits and back to the living. They entered a room whose walls were filled with lacy webs of minerals that had been embellished by an Indian hand. Simple, primitive drawings were traced on the walls of the room. Murals chiseled by flint and rock depicted figures stalking, tracking, and killing enemies and game. An almost lifesize bison gazed down at them, its eyes a gleaming yellow, its stone hide rich in the bronze and copper ores of the earth.

Geronimo paused briefly in the room as if to pay the respect demanded. Then with the others following closely behind, he passed under a huge stone archway. The forms on it were human and animal mixed. The faces which loomed down were grotesque and omnipotent. With deference, the party passed under the Arch of the Gods and continued silently off into the dark.

After many hours of travailing the turning, narrow crawlways, which were barely large enough for the horses, they arrived at a large chamber. In the center was a cool, bottomless pool. They would rest here. Taza sprawled on a rock in pain. His exhaustion had caught up with him. White Horse and Naiche started unloading dried leaves and twigs from one of the horses. They needed fire in the caves. Fire would not burn wet wood. They had come prepared. White Horse knelt before the pile of kindling. In a short while, they were bathed in shades of orange and blue light.

Geronimo sat off from the others. His rifle was braced over his knees. His forehead was clenched in a perpetual frown, which pinched his eyebrows closely together. He was tired, but his body did not slump. Unbeaten and unbroken, only his cunning had kept him alive. Two black eyes stared wearily before him. Remembering what? Alope, his young wife who had borne him three strong sons? Dead for more than twenty years. Janos, the Mexican town that had brutally cut her down with his sons and his aged mother. His eyes narrowed. The scars were old, but the pain was still there. It had started then—the wars, the running, the prisons. He blinked, trying to eradicate their memories. His face became calm, his eyes distant. He continued to stare off into the serene dark. Seeing what? Perhaps, his own death. . . .

Miles above the unvanquished, old warrior, the cavalry was making a rough camp. Lieutenant Bernard had been left to organize the detail. Several troopers were stringing rope along stakes in the ground in the center of which were the horses. The makeshift remuda was a churning bowl as hooves stirred up the thick layers of soot. Other soldiers were grazing horses by twos near the sides of the nearly perpendicular walls of the canyon. There was little forage for the animals.

Their muzzles pushed through stone and dirt in search of thin, dried blades of grass. Cactus and prickly pears abounded, but their spines made them inedible.

Huddled in the center were the civilians. Some were nibbling on jerky and hardtack. But for the most part, they sat numbly still, dazed by the events that had brought them to this baneful gorge. They apprehensively clutched their possessions as if expecting someone to steal them. Even the inviting sounds of Corporal Gatewood setting up the kitchen elicited no response. His big, black hands deftly handled the heavy iron pans. His fingers were nimble and quick. As a growing boy back in the small town of Valdosta, Georgia, he had learned to cook almost before he was allowed out. Twenty-three of his brothers, sisters, and cousins had worked Mr. Thurston Jason's eight-acre sharecrop to extinction. When Momma Florabelle had choked to death on a chicken bone, the ten-year-old slave had been sent to West Virginia, to Mr. Jason's second cousin, James Oliver Brandywine, who had put him in the livery.

He had slated steel plates onto horses twelve hours a day, seven days a week, building both muscle and hate for Mr. Jason's cousin. At fourteen, big for his age, he took off on one of the horses and rode clear to Pennsylvania, where he had lied his way into the army, using the forged signature of an old aunt to aid him. When asked what he liked to do best, Gatewood had replied, "eat," so into the kitchen he went. By twenty-two, he had achieved distinction for a black— promotion to corporal. He had found a niche in a white world. He had never stopped eating—privilege of being cook—and weighed almost three hundred pounds when he had arrived at his full growth, of which, the major said, "One hundred pounds was heart."

A short distance from the camp, the major led his horse along the sides of the walls. He was still scanning the cliffs for an answer to the mystery. Walking beside him was Joshua Barrett.

Scaling and climbing the rocks above them was Dull Knife, the cavalry scout. His wiry frame was encased in bits and remnants of cast-off uniforms. He moved agilely and recklessly. Slipping at times, he unleashed a steady stream of rocks and dirt, which splattered in front of the major and Barrett.

"Further over, Scout! There's nothin' there but lizards!" He squinted from beneath his hands, which shaded his eyes. His voice was thrown back by the walls. "That damn Dull Knife, he only understands shouting."

"Isn't this chancy, Major? Couldn't this be an ambush?"

"That's what I thought at first, too. But if it were, we'd had it by now. No, Mr. Barrett—we been here all day, and I haven't seen nothin' but horses' asses and snakes."

"What about tonight—when we're sleeping?"

"Not Apaches—they sleep at night. Lemme tell you, Barrett—I've been in this country so long that when I came here, Pike's Peak was just a hole in the ground, but I never saw the likes of this. We're camping right here till I figure it out. I'm not goin' back to Fort Huachuca without Geronimo's scalp."

"Then, I suppose," Barrett said cynically, "you'll get promoted to colonel?"

"Unfortunately, that won't make much difference. I've killed over one hundred braves since '69. I was a captain five, long years. Been a major seven. I put my life on the line for seventeen hundred bucks a year. Piss most of it away on liquor, women, and cards. Won't never be a colonel, friend—not long as I'm judged by the back-slapping, ass-kissin' bunch from the Point. Got no education. Quit school in the fifth grade to join up. Worked my way up from the ranks by my own bootstraps. There isn't any promotion for me this side of heaven." He spat into the dirt derisively.

Barrett took his notebook out of his pocket and made

a note. "Can I quote you?"

"Not on your life. I have one year to retire." He thrust his hand with middle finger extended toward the rim of the canyon. "Then, up the generals' asses!" The major motioned the scout on. "I've been after Geronimo's craggy hide for nine years now. He's fifty-five. I'm forty-one. I killed two of his cousins—one with my bare hands. The other with my gun. What do I have to gain, Mr. Barrett? You tell me!"

"Twenty thousand dollars, government reward?" Barrett asked with a cool edge, as he continued making notes.

The normal price for an Indian scalp was one hundred dollars in gold and silver. But Geronimo was special. His stealing of cattle alone had mounted into the tens of thousands, not to mention the path of blood that followed his trail. At first the army, by special dispensation from the Congress, had issued a five-thousand-dollar reward for him, dead or alive. But none were able to claim it. Ten years later, a Special Congressional Committee on Indian Affairs had upped the ante four times to the stupendous twenty-thousand figure, the condition of being alive or dead immaterial. Bounty hunters were incited, but their efforts were futile. Then the offer was expanded to include even the military. The major knew that twenty thousand dollars was all a man ever needed to live out the rest of his days in luxury. The sad face of the old warrior, Geronimo, lips grim, beaten down by time, appeared on a poster at every fort in the West, with the prominent reward over his head.

The major shrugged, "Well, there's that. I could go back to the Blue Grass State and buy back my family's horse ranch with that reward. Could be a colonel at last." He laughed, cynically. "A Kentucky colonel!"

"Is that what's been driving you, Major?"

"Money and blood, Mr. Barrett." He scanned the mountains thoughtfully. When he spoke, his voice was low, tinged with pain. "I'll do to him what he did to those three troopers back at Mogollon Plateau last winter."

"What was that, Major?"

"He hung them upside down over a fire and burned off their skin!"

"Weren't they the ones that killed fifteen squaws and children?"

"Same ones."

"Well, I suppose to him it seemed justified."

"Don't tell me about Apaches, Barrett," the major concluded, "they've been my life's work."

In order to do his Geronimo story, Barrett had had to use all his influence, which was considerable. An interview had been arranged with the Secretary of Indian Affairs, and through him, a letter had been procured from the president of the United States, Chester Alan Arthur. The document, signed in a big, fluid scrawl over the president's seal had stood him well. It had gained him admission to the West through the commanding officer of Fort Huachuca.

But it had not impressed the major who was suspicious—with good reason—of any kind of political epistles. Politics had kept him a major for far too many years. As far as he was concerned, politics had cut up the West to the benefit of the have-gots and to the dismay of the have-nots. It was politics that had lost his family their ranch in Kentucky: It had been the bane of his career and his life. Politicians used words as a smoke screen for their greed. Here it was again—more political horseshit. Why was this man Barrett from the East so damn intent on writing Geronimo's story? What was in it for him? The major could not help being highly suspicious. As he had told the sergeant, "I couldn't care less if the letter had come from Jesus Christ himself."

The major stared at Barrett. "The president of the U.S.A. doesn't know sweet Fanny Adam about Apaches, Arizona, or the army. Hell, he hasn't even been west of the Mississippi. From what I hear, all he knows about is teaching school. And don't put down a word of that!"

"All right, Major. I'm not here to get your story—but, as my letter states, Geronimo's—for the president."

"I thought you worked for the *St. Louis Star Dispatch?*"

"I work for both on this story, Major."

"Well, just get the facts straight on me."

Barrett added judiciously, "But I have." He read from his notebook. "Major Emmett Pilcher is one of the West's most celebrated Indian fighters. He rides like a Mexican, trails like an Apache, and shoots like a Kentuckian!" He paused, a wry smile spreading over his face. "How's that?"

Eli Fly, the photographer, set the match to a magnesium flare. After a tremendous flash, which spooked the major's horse, Mr. Fly emerged from under the camera's hooded tripod. He was a little gnat of a man. A battered derby hat tilted on his head. A gnawed cigar was stuck in his goat's face. "Thank you, Major."

Mr. Fly had been brought into the picture by Barrett. They had worked together on many stories—in New York and in Washington. Barrett had brought him to St. Louis over the proposed Geronimo series, which he promised would be the zenith of their careers. The wizened little Eli Fly's signature was scrawled under some of the great picture epics of the time. During the Civil War he had been on the front lines—where he had first encountered Barrett. His heart-rending photos were history now—stills that caught the war between the states. Graphic records of the event and the personal statements of a man tiny in physique, they were stamped with an extraordinary genius.

He had photographed the president of the United States. His camera had even caught the assassination of Lincoln. Now, he hoped to document the end of an era epitomized by the downfall of the great Apache warrior who had become a household word in the land,

33

Geronimo, himself. The major nodded as he tried to calm his horse. "Now all we need is a photo of Geronimo, sir."

"You'll get it, Mr. Fly." The major took out his pistol and twirled the Colt in one hand. "Alive or dead, I promise you. God created man, but Colonel Colt made him equal!" He then fired three times into the air and yelled, "Geronimo!" His voice, like a war cry, echoed against the canyon walls. The word *Geronimo* bounced from hollow to hollow and then died.

Chapter
Four

Far inside the Caves, the major's cry seeped down into the earth. *Geronimo* oozed into the chamber that housed the Indians' campfire. It now sounded more like a plaintive wail than a challenge. Hearing the call, Geronimo muttered. The others watched him as he picked up a live bat. It fluttered in his hand. He spread its wings and quickly speared it with a sharp wooden stake. He paused to listen, but the sounds had faded. Lifting the skewered bat, he pushed it into the flames and watched it roast.

A large fire raged in the camp. On it was an iron kettle of steaming coffee and a boiling pot of beans. Corporal Gatewood leaned into the savory aroma. He sniffed the bean mash as though it were the most delicious stew. Behind him, strung up on a pole was a side of bacon and slices of hardtack. Satisfied after a taste he turned to an iron triangle hung from a dead tree. The clanging brought life to the camp. Troopers, tin pans in hand, came trotting over from their resting places. The group of civilians stirred. They would be last in line and began rummaging through their boxes and bags for plates. The civilians had not eaten all day. The last time they had had a campfire was when the Apaches had obliged them to stop for a night.

The entire company was hunched over their pans spooning beans and corn as quickly as possible into their ravenous stomachs. Barrett, with Fly scuffling behind him, joined the line of rowdy soldiers.

Corporal Clay, a red-faced southern boy, turned to Fly. "Gatewood's the onliest black boy in the whole

Fourth Cavalry. He's all by hisself."

Private Hicks put down his pan and drawled, "Y'all know what they say about monkeys?"

"Nah, what's that, Hicks?" asked Clay.

"The higher they climb," he paused, "the more they show their asses!" They all had a laugh.

The tall, solid black man grinned with the rest of them. Then slowly as he stirred the beans, he said, "Tell y'what I'm gonna do, boys. You quit joshin' me, and I'll quit peeing in the soup."

Spitting out his mash, Orley cried, "Damn!" A few howls went down the line. Barrett hesitated before the bubbling pot. Gatewood winked at him and said, "Only fools pull the leg of a skunk, a mule, or a cook!" Barrett smiled at him not too sure about the mash in his pan. Mr. Fly decided to pass it up and filled his plate with several bacon ends and a hunk of sourdough.

The major had found himself a comfortable rock. He was hunched on it and gnawed at a ham hock. He had not been hungry until he had started eating. Now the days of chase had caught up to him. He had momentarily forgotten his acute disappointment. As he ate, his eyes scanned over the motley group assembled below him.

Barrett waded through the throng of sprawled bodies. No one paid him any attention. They were all too absorbed in quieting their own growling bellies. Barrett sat next to the major. Both stared down at the fire and ate.

"What do you know about old Judge Bedediah Tasker over there, Major?" Barrett finally broke the silence.

The major looked at Barrett, then turned his gaze on the judge. "Well, he isn't nicknamed 'Old Necessity' for nothing." He paused and looked at Barrett with bemused contempt as Barrett put down his food and started making notes again. He viewed the reporter half with scorn and half bewilderment. He then turned his attention back to the judge. "He's more crook than law keeper. He drinks like a fish, dresses like a deacon, and lives like a gambler." He laughed to himself, as he saw Barrett scribbling down his every word.

"I say bless the boys in blue!" Judge Bedediah Tasker toasted from his canteen. He was none too sober, and had not been since the cavalry had picked him up horseless and senseless twenty miles south of Tombstone. No one was sure how he had gotten there. The judge was a weasel-faced, slight man, with a perpetual liquor stench. He was a salted product of the West, a drifter and a con man of some repute. He swore—and none could prove otherwise—that he once was indeed a judge, holding court in a dilapidated saloon in Chaparral County in Southwest Texas. He had followed the railroad west, working the small towns, playing poker sometimes, or posing as a traveling deacon, speculating in land investment, mines, and such. He carried a briefcase full of deeds to nonexistent lands in faraway places, defunct gold stock certificates, and doubtful claims. He had smuggled liquor to the Indians, but drank up the profits. Once he had won seventeen thousand dollars in a forty-eight-hour poker play-out from a farmer who unfortunately died at the table from a heart attack before the good judge could collect. But he tried to no avail to collect from the farmer's widow. He wrote the summons himself, which was shortly thrown out of court.

Judge Tasker had no education whatsoever; he was totally self-taught. He carried a college degree and a justice of the peace license with him at all times. Because of his reputation, he was once hauled into a small saloon in Kansas and made to judge the kangaroo trial of an old Irishman for the killing of a Chinese laborer, with the clear warning that if the Irishman was found guilty, Judge Tasker would be hung with him. The good judge thumbed through his law books and finally decreed he could find no law that said a Chinaman couldn't be killed in Kansas. Drinks were had by all.

"Bullets will kill you," he exhorted, "but liquor is quicker!" He slugged back a quarter of his pint, winking and toasting the soldiers, especially the major.

Old Gabe grabbed the canteen from the judge and drank. Gabe had a face like a horned lizard. From a distance he could have been easily mistaken for a barrel cactus. "The way I figure it," he said, "man's the only animal that can be skinned more than once."

"Gabe," the sergeant asked, "how in hell can you make a livin' out of scalping Indians?"

"When the government stops paying me—I'll stop scalping!" Gabe spat into the fire.

"You don't even kill them though, do you?"

"I leave the killin' to you soldier boys, Sergeant. All I do is follow your bloody trails with my trusty hatchet."

"Like a vulture," the sergeant added. Then he asked, "How much did you make last year, Gabe?"

"Lemme see," Gabe began adding on his discolored fingers. "There was about twenty braves, maybe a coupla dozen squaws and little ones. What's that? About three thousand?"

"Hell, man—" the sergeant scoffed, "I only make seventeen dollars a month. I bet I killed more Indians last year than General Custer and I haven't seen a penny for it!"

"What's the good of killin' 'em, Sergeant, if you don't scalp 'em?"

"I heard that Geronimo put a bounty out for your scalp. Is that right, Gabe?"

"Yes. *Five* ponies!" Gabe said proudly. Gabe had come too close, too often, to losing his hair to the Apaches. Like a mongrel dog, he preferred his own company to city life and ways. Having long since abandoned the conventions of society, Gabe put little worth in the merits of his fellow man. Scalping—after a lifetime of failure—had become a way of life to Gabe. He was an artist, quick and efficient—seven or eight deft strokes and he could lift off the whole top of a head. These he dried in the sun and packed to keep, returning to the fort every couple of months, when he had enough for a decent payment. The Indians hated him and swore one day to get him. He was to them more than just a scavenger, but a vision of Death itself. He had not set the prices, he was just the tool of the government's laws. When the laws changed, so would he. He was cheerful in his work and resigned to his fate. He did not kill, he merely benefited from the bloody work of others. He followed the battles like a jackal, a coyote, a bird of prey—descending on the dying to ease them from their pain—and the already dead, to profit by them.

To the Indians, the scalp was a symbol of honor, to Old Gabe, it was just business. One day, if they caught him, he knew his own death would be too horrible to believe. Like John Pilthe, the infamous scalper from the Black Hills, he would be skinned and picked clean while still alive. Scalping would be left for last. They would smoke him first, then the hatchet. He knew he would still live through a few hours of torture before being relieved of his pain. The Apaches knew too well the art of that. So it was, Old Gabe hugged to the cavalry's side for fear of his fate. He never traveled alone. But then Death never did.

The sun's few remaining streaks filled the skies above the canyon in bold slashes of blues and reds. The desert cold would soon be upon them. It was a strange land of extremes. There was nothing temperate about it or its people. A man would burn during the day and then a few hours later feel a chill as cold as death's. Sergeant Talbot circled the camp, checking to see that there was enough firewood to last out the night. The civilians had already consumed half their supply. Their fire was roaring and stoked far too high. Cursing under his breath, he aroused two soldiers and sent them off for more wood.

As Talbot walked the perimeter, he kept nervously scanning the ridges for movement. As far as he was concerned, they were too much in the open. Once the civilians had bedded down, there had been no moving them. He, for one, would sleep closer to the walls.

The two women were huddled close to the fire. Baby Doe Tabber was a comely woman in her mid-thirties. The sun had not touched her soft, pallid complexion. Her fair skin was an oddity in the dirt-brown desert. She was dressed in the remains of a once-regal outfit. It was not a frontier dress or in any way practical. Its stays pushed and pulled her already voluptuous body.

"From rags to riches and back to rags, that's the story of my life, Mrs. Ducks." Baby Doe patted the case she was sitting on. The remnants of her great wealth—boxes, suitcases, and bulging sacks were all around her on the ground. "I got the remains of my great fortune on the back of one jackass."

Mrs. Ducks, a shriveled old woman with lines as deep as desert ravines in her face, eyed Baby Doe hostilely. Her calico dress and severe hairdo contrasted sharply with the younger woman. "You a fancy woman, Mrs. Tabber?"

Baby Doe laughed. "I never sell it, if that's what you mean, Mrs. Ducks. I only marry it off—"

"Same thing to some!" Mrs. Ducks bristled.

But that was not so to Baby Doe, who was born Margaret Stallmayer. From earliest age, her large doelike eyes had been appealing to men who gave her her name. Baby Doe had made marriage her career. She had had five marriages and three divorces. One had died and the other she had just not bothered to legally separate from. They were her secrets and who they were she was determined to take with her to her grave. But William K. Tabber, Bill, was the highlight of her life. When she had met him, he was married to a dour woman, an exboardinghouse keeper. The woman was psychotic about poverty and refused to help him spend his newly acquired millions after spending fifteen years with him in the dry mine fields of Colorado.

Bill had bought his way into the legendary Little Pittsburgh Silver Quartz Mine with seventeen dollars worth of provisions. He had profited to the tune of five hundred thousand. From then on, his luck was in. He had gone from mine to mine, each more lucrative than the last, accumulating millions—and Baby Doe. Ultimately, he discovered his political ambition and bought his way from mayor of Leadville to lieutenant governor of the territory.

He had abandoned his poverty-struck wife, divorced her, and had married Margaret Stallmayer who had no inclinations to save him a dime. He had lavished millions on her, including buying her carriages to match her dresses. She had selected her horses to complement her outfits and her moods. Bays, blacks, browns—with colorful plumes and harnesses. They had given incredible receptions in Washington.

He had bought Willard's Hotel and he and Baby Doe entertained the president there. Bill bought her two opera houses, one in Leadville, one in Denver, costing a million dollars each. Baby Doe had been thrilled—she was the toast of Denver. She pointed proudly to the portrait of William Shakespeare in the lobby, about which the poorly educated Bill had asked, "Who the devil is that?" She had replied, "William Shakespeare!" "William Shakespeare?" Bill had cried. "What the hell did he ever do for Denver? Take down his pitcher and put mine there!"

She had. But, when the price of silver had plummeted, so had Bill's fortune—and Baby Doe's. All, all had to be sold, and death claimed what had been left from Bill's estate As for Baby Doe, she fled from creditors with the last remains of her past splendor carefully packed in two huge suitcases. Now, bereft, lost, alone for the first time in her life—a life dependent wholly on men—she suffered the final ignominy of her flight: an Apache raid and a rescue by the cavalry. Such was her life. She stared in some confusion at the plain, simple face of the farmer's wife before her. She was not even sure of the woman's name, less her reality, or much less her own at that moment either.

The weathered old farmer's wife took out some sewing. Her face bunched up like a warthog as she squinted in the diminishing light. Mrs. Ducks had only known the hard life of the land. They'd built and lost over a dozen farms in twenty years. Her father had been a man of God in Indiana. She'd been weaned on the Bible. Faith was her rock, her foundation. The course of her suffering had been a test for her and for her husband, Sidney. They had suffered but had not been found wanting. She was certain after this, the supreme test, that things would be better. She prayed with the conviction of a Saint. She suffered in silence. If death was to be her only salvation, so be it. It was the ultimate test she was sure, and she was ready. As she sewed, she prayed, the words running around in her brain, a litany of love for her God, first, and her husband, second.

Baby Doe looked off toward the tent beside which the major was grazing his horse. She said under her breath, more to herself than anyone, "That major sure is married to the army, isn't he?" There was a look of wonder in her face, perhaps even a curious thought.

The major took his horse a short distance from the camp to find better forage. He had brought the large gray from Kentucky. It was the last horse from the pure line that his father had bred. All the others had been conscripted during the war and were by now either dead or behind a plow or worse. Dynamite, as the major called the animal, was like a child to him—his only son. He bedded the horse down. Then, he returned to the edge of the camp. Stopping in the shadows, he watched as Baby Doe settled down for the night. The fire lit her face, making the skin and hair glow. The burnt-orange wavering light made her features sharper and more defined. He thought she was a dandy woman, all right.

She crawled under her blankets and squirmed away rocks and twigs with her back. The major waited until there was no movement around the campfire. He then wearily returned to his tent.

Waiting for him there was Barrett, Fly, and Lieutenat Bernard. Bernard quickly rose as he entered. Barrett smoked a pipe, Fly polished a lens.

"Lieutenant, where's my whiskey?" The lieutenant quickly turned, left the tent, and could be heard rummaging in a box outside. He soon reappeared with a bottle and handed it to him. The major put it down as he continued to unbutton his shirt. He wiped his hands on his pants to clean some of the dirt off of them. "Wesley, get me some water—my skin's like to crawl off me and die."

Again the lieutenant left and returned with a bucket. Major Pilcher was much amused by the young lieutenant. He tried not to abuse the boy, though often he found himself doing just that. The lieutenant liked the major, liked his rough hue, his western machismo—but it was a bitch putting up with his patronizing attitude. The lieutenant retreated into submissiveness, upstaged not so much by rank, but by the major's conciliatory manner. Even the sergeant fared better. But then he and the major had been together for years. He felt the major and the sergeant were one and the same. The sergeant was the voice of the major; he had the king's ear, so to speak. Bernard bit his lip, cursed his wayward ways, and waited to gain more experience. After all, he had been there less than a year. The two old soldiers had a lifetime of experience ahead of him. He stared at the major fiddling with his tin cup.

The major disregarded this, poured a dollop of liquor into a steaming mug of coffee. He looked at Barrett pensively. Sticking a chewed cigar into his mouth, he let it dangle there for several seconds. "When I was first sent west, I was a sergeant." He stirred the liquor with one crusted finger. "One of my first jobs was to teach Apache prisoners English. Well, the bastards tricked me right from the start—they taught *me* Apache instead!"

"Well, they always say it's good to have another language, Major," Barrett needled him.

"Geronimo did most of his running with Magnus Coloradas coupla hundred miles east of here near Taos and south in Mexico, till Coloradas died."

"Wasn't Magnus Coloradas promised peace and when he came in, the soldiers killed him?"

"Don't know where you get your facts, Barrett. Sure, he came into Fort Bowie, saying he was all for peace. But he was so drunk they had to put him in the guardhouse for safe keeping. And old Coloradas up and almost killed two troopers trying to escape. He would've made it—except for five bullets in his back." Barrett eyed the major skeptically. "The fact is Geronimo is the last great Indian warrior left. Coloradas, Cochise, Crazy Horse—they're all dead. Hell, Geronimo's escaped from four reservations. If you put him in a room with no doors, he'd find a way out. Get him and you've got them all."

"What about the treaties the army broke?"

"I didn't. Those damn West Point generals did." He added cynically, "They weren't treaties—they were tricks." The major looked up and speculated. "For years we've been damn mystified as to where in hell Geronimo's been taking the horses and cattle he stole. Hell, one night a couple years ago, he stole all our horses while we were sleeping. We never heard a sound. He's like a ghost—hits, raids, burns, and runs. Can't tag him. I guess somewhere in this canyon is where he comes. If you ask me, we've stumbled onto his secret headquarters."

"But, there are no signs of any fires. No old campsites. Nothing?" the lieutenant questioned.

Barrett flipped the page of his notebook, already having filled several sheets during the course of the evening.

The major nodded. "Up until today—nobody ever

44

thought this canyon existed except in Apache legends." Barrett continued writing. "Well, Dull Knife told me this canyon is only half of the legend—the rest of it's about a giant cave—nine, ten, eleven miles long!"

Bernard whistled, "Why—that'd mean if the mouth was here in Arizona. . . ."

"The ass would be in Mexico," the major finished. He poured more whiskey into his coffee, his final nightcap.

The blazing early sun bathed the canyon walls in cold hues of purple. As the sun climbed into the sky, the shadows slowly crept away from the sleeping camp. Steamy mist quickly evaporated as the morning heat filtered across the camp. Dozens of huddled, blanket-wrapped figures dotted the floor of the canyon. The only movements were two sleepy soldiers who marched along the edges of a makeshift log barricade. As the sun scorched their faces, one of the soldiers took out of his belt a bent and dented bugle.

Major Pilcher scrambled down the small rise toward the lean-to that Corporal Gatewood had erected as the mess tent. A brewing iron kettle of coffee was already on the fire. The major quickly poured himself a cup and downed it. As he waited for the effects to take hold, he surveyed the walls surrounding them. He was as baffled as ever.

Sergeant Talbot passed the major without a word and shakily got himself a boiling cup of the redemptive brew. He mumbled something as his lips hung over the rim of the metal cup. The major ignored it.

"I want you to detail all the men to scour this damn canyon till we find where the hell Geronimo disappeared!" He refilled his tin mug. "You see Dull Knife?"

"Not since last night. Think he slept with the horses."

"See if you can find the son of a bitch!" said the major, cup in hand, as he headed back toward his tent. He prided himself in being able to think like an Apache and had often second-guessed them. It was unlike Geronimo to set a trap and not use it immediately. He had to dismiss the idea of ambush, but the thought still troubled him. Not finding that cave was like wandering in some diabolical purgatory—or losing his mind.

Hours later, the major sat on his horse and watched the figures of Dull Knife and half a dozen soldiers grow smaller as they scaled the sides of the canyon. They had been searching all morning and most of the afternoon. Nothing except lizards and scorpions had been turned up. Now as they gleaned the other side of the gorge, the major's nerve ends were frayed. He sweated like a pig. His agitation went down the reins to his horse, which was fidgeting and skittish. Its hooves kicked up loose gravel and rocks as they climbed up a sharp embankment on top of which Sergeant Talbot stood watching Dull Knife above him.

Suddenly, the Indian disappeared from view. Thirty long seconds went by. The major mused, "What the hell happened to that addle-brained scout. He hasn't got any tiswin with him, has he?"

They had found that their half-breed strayed less from his duties if he was given a small supply of liquor each night. The Mexicans had made him an alcoholic, the cavalry kept him that way.

"Maybe I better go up there—" The sergeant stopped.

Dull Knife reappeared, waving and yowling excitedly down to them. He quickly clambered down the steep cliff, starting a small landslide of stones before him. Both men instantly spurred their horses.They rode as far up as they could go, then dismounted and scrambled up to join the scout.

Dull Knife led them to a huge overhang. It was almost entirely hidden by a rock formation in front of it. A twisting path was pressed between the boulders. There was room enough for one horse—no more—to edge its way past the rocks and under the ledge. To one side of the overhang, a path had been chipped out of the granite. It was almost five feet wide—enough to enable a horse to get through. A cave! Both men stood at the entrance with exuberant, transfixed stares. Dull Knife stood somewhat behind them, looking into the hole apprehensively.

Chapter Five

"**J**esus H. Christ!" The sergeant let out a low, reverent whistle.

"Well, Talbot—this is it." Major Pilcher spoke without taking his eyes off the mouth of the Cave. Dull Knife began talking rapidly in Apache. His first few words went unheard by the major. Finally the scout pulled his arm to get attention, motioned, and gesticulated fearfully.

"Dull Knife says they came this way. The ponies' tracks were covered, but no matter, he found signs. It's a big cave, all right." The scout interrupted, shook his head. "He says he won't go in."

It was one thing being an Indian scout working with the white soldiers, but this cave was deep in sacred Apache territory. Dull Knife did not like their chances. What would happen to him if caught he knew too well. In the Caves he was sure was the great warrior himself and three of his best braves. No, he would not go in. If there was a price on Geronimo's head, there was a curse on his, an ancient and powerful curse.

"What's wrong with him?"

Again came the rapid interchange of the soft guttural language between the two men. Dull Knife crouched on his heels and waited.

"He says in the Cave, the White Man got no chance at all. Inside is certain death."

"We goin' in?"

"We'll just explore the mouth with a few troopers. We'll need a torch." He turned to face the scout. "Dull Knife's going in, if I have to drag him by his asshole. If he don't, I'm throwing him back into the stockade where I found him." He quickly translated this threat to the Apache.

The sergeant went to the edge of the ledge and called down. "Orley, Yager, Hicks! Come with me." The soldiers started up the rocky precipice.

"And get the lieutenant up here," the major called over as he peered into the hole.

A few minutes later, Bernard came running up to him, excited and out of breath. "Wesley, I want you to take charge out here. If I call, come runnin' with all the muster we have! You, Clay, Slack and Gatewood—stay by the lieutenant, rifles at the ready. Hear?"

The path into the mountain twisted narrowly for the first hundred feet. It hugged the south side of the overhang. To their right, the giant slabs of granite pressed against each other tightly. Only a scant few feet were between the rocks—barely enough room for a horse and a man to crawl. The chiseled walkway had been worn by time—centuries old. Slowly, imperceptibly, the path began to angle down. The slant became sharper as the floor and ceiling moved apart. Then, without warning, the torch flared up to reveal an immense chamber. The major stopped abruptly. He stepped back unconsciously a few feet. The others, behind him, hugged the sides of the wall looking out into the vast open area in awe. The enormity of the room and its splendor was breathtaking.

"Look at those rocks!" The major's voice was muted, "Like damn icicles hanging from the roof!" He moved out into the open, gazing at the huge stalactites.

"Major . . . " the sergeant whispered hoarsely, "what if the Apaches are here?"

"They're not within five hundred yards, Talbot." He moved further into the cave. "I would've smelled them if they were."

After they had been out in the open and not fired upon, the party moved easier. Their voices echoed softly in the hollow, damp chamber.

"Look at those jaggedy things comin' up from the

floor!" Orley stammered. "Must be eighty, ninety feet!"

The major walked back to Talbot who carried the torch. "Must be miles and miles of caverns in here—what else can you see, Sergeant?"

"Looks like pools of water, over there," he pointed with the torch.

"Looks like the Gates of Hell to me," Orley mumbled. His grandma had always sworn to him as a boy—if he saw the Gates of Hell he would be stupid enough to walk through. Well, in his mind's eye there were those very gates—but he wasn't taking one step.

Suddenly, the cavern was filled with a tremendous, swirling roar. "What the hell is that!?" The group pulled together. Their eyes darted around the semi-lit walls. The major cocked his pistol. Sergeant Talbot held the torch high above his head.

"Jesus!" The high, chirping cries and rushing air swelled wildly. "Bats!" The bats blinded by the condensed light of the torch, swirled around them.

"Droves of the blood-suckin' devils!"

"Don't let them get in your hair, Major!"

"Just keep the torch moving—that'll keep them off!"

Thousands of bats crushed the air. The sound grew until it was a cacophony of ear-piercing dissonance. Private Orley, in panic, fired his rifle at the teeming hoard. The shot split through the room, echoing and reverberating again and again.

The major whirled around. "What the hell are you doing, man?" Orley said nothing in reply. He merely trembled.

Seeing something, Dull Knife scampered ahead and knelt on the stone floor.

"Bat bones. Fresh. Eaten," the major said as he bent down over a small heap of tiny bones.

Slowly, distantly the low rumble of tom-toms came from deep inside the cave. It drifted in from one direction, then another. The small party stared at each other. Their eyes tried to follow the sounds, which echoed and re-echoed in the darkness and around them. Suddenly, the drums stopped. Only the men's measured breathing could be heard. Even the bats had stopped churning. The cave was engulfed in silence. An animal shriek ripped through the room—or was it Indian? Like a wild bird, it cried mournfully, almost in pain. The major, Sergeant Talbot and the scout and the others instinctively began to back out. . . .

The major and his party wearily slunk out of the Caves. The sun, low on the canyon's rim, was blinding. They all stood for a moment, blinking against the sharp contrast to the Cave's dark. Then Dull Knife began to grumble in Apache. The major's squint changed to a dark scowl.

"What's he say?" Sergeant Talbot asked. He shielded his eyes with his hands. The setting un's intensity was painful.

"He's not going back in the Caves tomorrow. He's decided to go back to the stockade; it's safer there."

The scout took a drink from his canteen, shifted, and turned his back to them. The major angrily kicked the canteen out of Dull Knife's hands. The Indian stood up in surprise.

"Before you go back to the stockade, I'll sell your scalp to Old Gabe!" For a moment the major had forgotten himself. The scout looked at him stupidly. Then the major began to rattle in Apache. Dull Knife listened, grunted, then spit out more words. Major Pilcher laughed derisively. "The scout says Geronimo will give five ponies for Gabe's scalp, but *ten* for mine!"

Above the entrance to the Caves, high up over Skeleton Canyon was a ledge. Only the bottom side of it could be seen from the floor of the canyon. A wolf was crouched on top of it. The animal's head slowly lifted—to reveal a face. A human face. The cold eyes of White Horse stared down without once blinking at every movement below. The blood ran icily through his

51

veins. He gazed at the intruders with black hate, which surged from the depths of his gall.

There was little excitement over the major's discovery among the civilians. If anything, they were disappointed that he had found the Caves. It meant that they would have to remain in the canyon longer than they had hoped. Their fatigue was more evident, even after a day of rest. For the most part, the group kept close to the campfire. There was little conversation that night. They were too uncomfortable to do little more than worry. It had been a day of uncompromising heat, which had left them depleted. No one did much of anything. Even the judge was quiet. He sulked, away from the others, seeking solace in a bottle. They were all dogged and tattered. A motley assortment of grimy clothes made them look more like scarecrows than human beings.

The judge and Venable had drained one bottle between them and were halfway through the second. Venable Brown looked like a heap of sorry desolation as he polished his mining pick and scratched caked mud from his old shovel. He squinted at the judge and asked, "Hey, judge, y'know the miner's Ten Commandments?"

"Nope," the judge belched back.

Venable was now smashed altogether. His sodden words began to spill out of his mouth to his audience scattered around the campfire. On shakey legs, he stood and began to rant: "One," he said wavering through the firelight, "Thou shalt have no other claim than one."

"There was a smattering of laughter at this. "That's rich!" the judge chortled.

"Two!" Venable went on, "Thou shalt not make unto thee self any false claim." There was no stopping him now. "Three, neither shalt thou take thy gold dust, nor thy good name to the gaming table in vain; for twenty-one, roulette, faro, and poker will prove to thee

52

that the more thou puttest down the less thou shalt take up." He drank and went on. "Four, six days thou mayest dig or pick all that thy body can stand under; but the other day is the Sabbath. Thou must not washest thy dirty shirts, darnest all thy stockings, tap thy boots, mend thy clothing, chop thy whole week's firewood, make up and bake thy bread, or boil thy pork and beans. The trader and the blacksmith, the carpenter and the merchant, the tailors, Jews, and buccaneers, defy God and civilization, by keeping not the Sabbath day, nor wish for a day of rest, such as memory, youth and home hath made hallowed.

Old Gabe sniggered. "Five?" he asked.

Venable plunged ahead. "Thou shalt not think more of all thy gold, and how thou canst make it fastest, than how thou wilt enjoy it, after thou hast ridden roughshod over thy good old neighbor—so desist!"

They were all listening now. "Six!" he thundered on. "Neither shalt thou kill thy neighbor's body in a duel. Neither shalt thy destroy thyself by getting tight nor slewed nor high nor corned nor three sheets in the wind by drinking smoothly down brandy slings, gin cocktails, whiskey punches, rum toddies nor egg nogs. Neither shalt thou suck mint juleps nor sherry cobblers through a straw, nor gurgle from a bottle the raw nor take it neat from a decanter; for thou art burning the coat from off thy stomach. Thou wilt feel disgusted with thyself and inquire, 'Is thy servant a dog that he doeth these things?' Verily, I will say, farewell, old bottle, I will kiss thy gurgling lips no more. And thou, slings, cocktails, punches, smashes, cobblers, nog, toddies, and juleps, forever farewell. Thy headaches, tremblings, heart burnings, blue devils, and all the unholy evils that follow in thy tram. My wife's smiles and my children's merry-hearted laughs, shalt charm and reward me for having the guts to say no. I wish thee farewell."

"Seven!" He was in his cups, on a stage, the frustrated actor of his youth. "Thou shalt not grow discouraged, not think of going home before thou hast made thy pile. Thou knowest by staying here, thou might strike a lead and fifty dollars a day, and keep thy manly self-respect, and then go home with enough to make thyself and others happy."

"Eight!" Venable roared on. "Thou shalt not steal a pick or a shovel or a pan from thy fellow miner, nor take away his tools without his leave; nor borrow those he cannot spare, nor return them broken, nor trouble him to fetch them back again, nor talk with him while his water is running on, nor remove his stake to enlarge thy claim, nor pan out gold from his box nor wash the tailings from his sluice's mouth. Neither shalt thou pick out bits from the company's pan to put them in thy mouth or in thy purse, nor cheat thy partner of his share. Nor steal from thy cabinmate his gold dust, to add to thine, for he will be sure to discover what thou hast done, and will straightway call his fellow miners together, and if the law hinder them not, they will hang thee or give thee fifty lashes or shave thy head and brand thee like a horse thief, with *T* upon thy cheek, to be known and read of all men, Californians in particular."

read of all men, Californians in particular."

They were spellbound. He continued after taking still another drink. "Nine! Thou shalt not tell any false tales about good diggins in the mountains to thy neighbor, that thou mayest benefit a friend who hath mules and provisions and blankets, he cannot sell— lest in fooling thy neighbor, when he comes through the snow, with naught save his rifle, he present thee with the contents thereof and like a dog thou shalt fall down and die."

Venable beat his chest like the hammy actor he was, rising to the climax. "Ten!" he shouted. "Thou shalt not commit matrimony, nor forget absent maidens, nor neglect thy first love, but thou shalt consider she awaiteth thy return. Yes, and covereth each letter that thou sendest with kisses. Neither shalt thou covet thy neighbor's wife, nor trifle with his daughter; yet, if thy

54

heart be free, and thou dost love each other, thou shalt pop the question like a man, lest another, should step in ahead of thee. Otherwise, such is life that thy future lot be that of a poor, lonely, despised, miserable, and comfortless bachelor like the one that you see here before you tonight—a confirmed drunk, a liar, and a fool." With that, Venable sat quietly—and finished the bottle. They stared at him in silence, awed by his performance and his sudden burst of utter honesty.

After his outburst, the camp seemed unearthly quiet. Only the soft treading of the sentries could be heard. Their steps were slow and strained. It was the last watch of the night. It was their luck that it had started to rain. The two soldiers pulled on their slickers and continued their lonely march around the camp. The rain began to come down harder.

The early morning light was diminished by thick, swirling clouds. Thunder rolled across the sky. The sentries glanced up nervously. The clouds were becoming blacker, more ominous.

The party began to stir. They groped around in their belongings for slickers to shield them from the annoying rain. The fire crackled and sizzled. It soon went out. Civilians and soldiers alike were cursing the sudden shift in the weather. They were groggy from an uneasy sleep. The drenching and their hunger made their tempers short and vitriolic. As a body they made their way for the mess tent where Corporal Gatewood was trying to restart the fire. They watched him impatiently as he wrestled with soggy wood and damp matches.

The clouds were dipping low into the canyon. The tops of the walls were obliterated. Strangely, the wind had died down. No one noticed; they were too intent on getting some coffee. Suddenly, the atmosphere became dead and stifling. It was as though the air had been sucked out beyond their reach. The clouds became yellow, puss yellow. All movement stopped.

"What is it?" Barrett tensed, ready to make for cover.

The major did not answer, but his eyes searched the skies. Coming over the rise and heading straight toward them was a monstrous swirl, a winding and blinding umult of trapped wind and sound—*a tornado!*

Chapter
Six

The fierce gale suddenly tore across the campsite. The major's tent was pulled up by the stakes and slung against the canyon walls like a newspaper.

"Tornado!" the major screamed, but his words were lost in the deafening roar. An enormous explosion ripped across the sky. Everyone below froze in their tracks. The major began to cry into the wind. "Start moving everyone into the Caves—move the supplies—hurry!"

The words were caught in the wind. The dark clouds swirled down, almost touching the floor of the camp. The sky crackled and burst with flashes of blue lightning. A whip of thunder resounded directly overhead. It echoed and re-echoed until the very earth seemed to tremble. Torrents and waves of biting water spewed down from the sky. The wind howled around the massive canyon. Gusts whipped around the curved walls, building into a gigantic whirlpool.

Pandemonium. Figures rushed everywhere. Confusion. Shouting. The horses were neighing in panic. They huddled together. Their hooves lashed out at anyone who tried to approach. The sky poured down, drenching objects and humans alike. Bodies, horses, equipment were being dragged frantically up and into the Caves.

Sergeant Talbot wiped the wet from his eyes, shielding them with his hands from the pelting fury. He spotted the gray, the major pulling his animal toward the hole. Man and animal alike moved blindly. The rain was driving bitterly in waves against them. The major whipped his horse across the flanks. The horse bolted forward and reared. The animals were in total panic. They careened dangerously between the rocks and up the narrow path that led to the rock shelter.

The canyon was tumultuous. Great clouds of powder exploded over its edges. The funnel lapped from side to side devouring tons of earth. The men below stared helplessly down into the inferno frozen by the storm. The wind became hail. Ice stones, some as big as glass eyes, spewed down on them. They scrambled up the path to the dark, foreboding shelter of the Caves.

Bolts of lightning ripped across the night sky. Quaking roars of thunder prodded the earth. The campsite disappeared.

Inside the mountain, the party waited it out. They were slowly recovering from their shock. Some of the soldiers were working over their packs, spreading things out to dry. Everything was drenched. Figures were fumbling about in the dark shadows of the cavern, trying to make the best of it. Food, ammunition, clothes were strewn all around them. Some were trying feebly to salvage their few possessions, which had been dumped haphazardly in their rush to refuge. The horses and mules were packed closely together in a corner near the mouth of the cave. They, like everyone else, were trying to fight off the bone-damp chill that penetrated to their marrow.

A meager fire burned. Over it, the kettle of coffee boiled. Gatewood handed out smouldering cups to the dozen or so figures who huddled around the flames. They sat closely, shoulders pressed against each other for warmth. Gatewood was as wet as the rest and as tired.

"Hell, this rainstorm ain't nothing. I once was in a twister that made this one look like dew." He looked around at the sullen faces. No one reacted to a word he had said.

Baby Doe clutched a blanket tightly around her shoulders. She sat close to the small fire, like a broken doll. Her streaked face glowed in the flickering light. The major, a few feet from her, turned and looked at her for a long moment.

"Just how did those Apaches ever miss the likes of you, Mrs. Tabber?"

Baby Doe's face managed a wet smile. "I was in the bushes, takin' care of nature when they came upon us, Major. I didn't move a hair, till you all rode up."

"Well, the rest of your party wasn't so lucky."

"No." She shook her head.

The major stared at her, then into the fire. Her closeness and femininity were disturbing. He coughed and cleared his throat awkwardly. "Mrs. Tabber? Your name sure rings a bell."

Despite the dirt and her depression, her eyes glowed alive. "Name's Margaret Stallmayer, but half a Augusta calls me Baby Doe. You musta heard of my late husband, Mr. Tabber. He went from postmaster to owner of the largest silver mine in the world."

"Sure. Now I remember. William K. Tabber."

"Bill's trouble started when he got political ambitions. One day I was a kept woman, next he made me a politician's wife, in satins and silks. Had five maids and a carriage for every day of the week!" Her tone became withdrawn again. "Unfortunately, Bill went bust, shot himself, and here I am." She paused, then added, "I'm a once in a lifetime bargain, goin' beging. . . ."

"Now, now, ma'am," the major comforted her.

"I'm afraid." She implored him with her eyes for strength. "I can't sleep. I'm afraid the Apaches in here will kill us for sure. God, help us!"

The major stared about in the quiet and dangerous darkness around them. "God help us all!" he muttered under his breath.

The major turned to jelly at the sight of a woman's helplessness. It welled up a great grief to him of another time, another woman. Of one long winter, when he had been fifteen. They had run off to the mountains to spend one summer together—a summer the likes of which he would never have again—but they had stayed too long. After summer, there was winter, winter with its icy winds from out of the mouth of Death.

Louise May Freshette had been his only love. They had married themselves in the dark, vast northern night. A month later, he had put her frail body to rest, just as Spring had broken the earth. The price in guilt he carried with him would never be discharged.

The fire flared up briefly. A log fell, sending up a few sparks. The heat began to fade. Those near the fire moved closer, their bodies slumped miserably.

"Give me the wood, Major, and I'll give you the fire," Gatewood lamented.

"All right, you people." A couple of blank faces blinked back. "Make yourselves useful—scare up some wood! There's plenty of it by the Caves' mouth. We'll watch for Apaches." They looked at him numbly. "Move!" They all listened nervously to the raging tempest outside. Their eyes were fixed vacantly on the darkness beyond.

Wet logs were soon smoking and sizzling in the flames. The party took less notice of the howling winds now that their stomachs were full. The day was slowly being forgotten.

The judge had found a bottle. He and a small group were clustered together drowning out the awful sounds from outside.

A great portion of their food supplies were gone. A number of saddles and rifles could not be accounted for. Several boxes of ammunition had been left behind and would be useless by now. They had been hit hard. It was worse than the sergeant had expected. They had just enough to get back to the fort. Even then, it would be rough going.

The major and two troopers were tending the horses. The animals had been badly shaken in the melee. They were full of cuts and scrapes. The major, to his dismay, had found an ugly gash on his gray. The animal favored one leg heavily. His careful hands worked to bind the wound.

Eli Fly sat off by himself amid a heap of bent and twisted photographic equipment. Months of work had been spoiled. He worked to salvage what he could.

Suddenly the horses began to mill around. Dynamite backed away from the major. Another animal reared up, its legs missing the major's head by inches. All of them were blowing and snorting in fright. Their panicked neighs brought some of the men running to their feet.

A stench of wet, rotten meat drifted into the Caves. A hoary growl came rumbling down the mouth of the entrance. Without warning, a snarling, soaking, angry, thousand-pound black bear loomed into view. People scattered before it.

The major cried out, "Talbot, a torch!" The sergeant raced to the fire. Then, moving with great caution, his torch held high, he approached the frightened beast as it lumbered down the entranceway. The animal, too, was running from the storm. The torch provoked him, making him frantic. He struck out at the fire with his great paws, dropped to his feet, and slunk off a short distance on all fours. Then, he loomed up again to his full height and charged.

The women screamed. Muffled, confused words from the men. Chaos and confusion. Everyone was trying to escape. Soldiers fired their weapons. Some were running directly into the line of fire. Bodies stumbled, fell and crawled. Horses hooves clashed against each other and stone. In the flickering light, the tormented bear rose up again. He stood on his hind legs and clawed the air. Then suddenly, the beast crashed into the neighing horses and screaming mules. Hooves struck out. The milling pile of flaying hooves and flesh quickly scattered. A mule lay at the bear's feet, its neck completely ripped open. The snarling, wild creature stood back. In his paws were hunks of dripping, raw flesh. He tore and ripped more meat off the dead carcass. In his hunger, he had fogotten the men.

Two shots rang out. They echoed crazily. A voice cried out, "Get the sonofabitch!"

The bear growled in surprise. He looked balefully around the cavern. Then, still clinging to his hunk of flesh, he began lumbering off in pain. He swayed clumsily and heavily off into the dark—and was gone.

Few of them were sleeping when the sun splintered over the ridge. Sometime during the night, the heart of the storm had passed. The unaccustomed quiet had made them all edgy. Knowing that the bear was somewhere nearby had kept them awake. The rain had diminished to a slight drizzle. The wind blew eerily over the canyon. Dark, gray storm clouds still swirled about, but began to scatter.

The major drew the lieutenant aside. "Wesley, nobody goes out unless *I* give the say so."

The lieutenant and more than a dozen soldiers left the cavern and rode up the mud-clogged entrance. A few of the civilians followed them curiously. The lieutenant waved them back. The soldiers, rifles and guns in evidence, clustered at the edge of the overhang. They scanned the canyon floor. It was a sea of uprooted cactus and floating waste. The camp was nowhere in sight. The major's tent was split, half plastered against a wall and half floating in a yellow pool of slime. Vultures stalked the ground. A black teeming hoard of the vicious birds had devoured one fallen horse. Its bones bobbed about in a black muddy pool. The birds were slitting another with talons and beaks. High above the sentries, unnoticed, waited the lone wolf.

The Apache, White Horse, had become the wolf—like a good actor, living his part. As a young brave, the Apache had prowled into a wolves' lair getting within twenty feet of the brood, before they had smelled what they could not see. He learned to howl like the animal, a howl he had nurtured for many days until it was as perfect as the real one. He could kill like the wolf—

often disguising his presence under the gray fur, to rise and fire at the swift antelope, moose, elk, or buffalo. But the animal the wolf hated today was the most dangerous of all—the white animal. The white animal was not ready, but the wolf was. . . .

The fire was big and smoky. Corporal Gatewood's hands worked rapidly over the slaughtered mule's carcass. Gatewood wore a white, bloodied apron. He deftly sliced the hide of the animal. In one tearing movement, he separated the skin from the purple flesh. He then proceeded to carve with the knife held tight in his red-drenched hands. He hacked off great hunks of mule. The others stared at him in horrible fascination.

"Well, the Lord, He tooketh Old Buckshot but He giveth us mule steak!" The meat sizzled and roasted noisily. The meat was stringy and had a peculiar flavor. Regardless, they ate it ravenously.

"As long as that bear's in here, none of us are safe. Besides, bear's food."

Dull Knife, the sergeant, and several soldiers followed the major deeper into the Caves. "Fan out—all of you—in a half circle, lads." They peered nervously beyond their torches. "Remember that beast isn't dead, just wounded!"

"Bugger the bear, Major," the sergeant yelled across to him. "I'm keeping wary of Apaches!"

"You can't *eat* Apache, Talbot." The major urged his skittish gray into the dark. The horse could smell the danger and sidled nervously along the path.

Suddenly, a chilling howl knifed through the canyon. The lieutenant and the other soldiers on guard looked up. Eli Fly, clutching his canvas-wrapped box camera and tripod, moved closer to the lieutenant. They scanned the canyon walls for the source of a wild animal.

The judge gathered up his heavy satchel and liquor and walked toward the cave entrance. He was stopped halfway out by Private Orley, rifle held before him.

"Can't go out!" The judge did not move. Orley prodded him with his rifle. "Go on back!"

The judge stood his ground. *"Who* says so, dammit?"

"Orders!"

"To hell with you and to hell with the major!"

"What do you want, Tasker?" the major asked him wearily from his horse. They had not found any sign of the bear.

"Out!"

"It's a lot easier keeping you all together in here, than out there," the major said simply.

"We ain't your prisoners, Major!" Venable Brown shouted. His years of penniless prospecting had caked layers of mining dirt under his fingernails, but no gold. His hands were permanently blackened. Not even a wire brush could scrape off those years of grime.

Bull Whacker, a greasy, one-eyed, glass-eyed cowboy, with a face like a tired saddle, always sided with the man who shouted the loudest. Drinking partners were hard to come by and the judge shared his bottle. Bull Whacker could not remember how many times he had been swindled by the army and their strict adherence to brand marks and the like. He had lost a good fifteen head of rustled Mexican steers to the damned quartermaster at Fort Huachuca just because he didn't have a bill of sale. As it turned out, he ended up with a mouth full of dust and a month gone to nothing.

The major walked slowly to the fire. His hands shook slightly as he poured himself a mug of coffee.

The judge was suddenly very unsure. He searched the sotted corners of his mind for something appropriate to say, but his thirst overtook him. Like a coyote with its tail between its legs, he slunk back into his bottle.

Again, the low, baneful cry of the wolf slipped around the canyon walls. The lieutenant still standing guard at the Caves' mouth suddenly spotted some movement above them.

"There's a wolf, Lieutenant!" Fly had seen it, too.

"Be quiet, Fly. Damn you!" The lieutenant quickly raised his rifle. He panned the rifle over the craggy range to the animal. He cocked the hammer carefully with his thumb and started to squeeze the trigger. Suddenly, it was not a wolf that he was aiming at, but the face and hands of an Apache. Clutched in the Indian's grip was a rifle. The lieutenant froze. He lowered his rifle, momentarily stunned. Then he hissed under his breath, "That ain't no wolf! It's Apache!" He quickly dropped down behind a rock. Eli Fly was nailed to the spot. His legs trembled uncontrollably. "Don't stand there with your finger in your ass, Fly—go tell the major. Get him quick, man!" Fly uprooted and fled inside the cave. "You soldiers, down!" The lieutenant whispered sharply back to the troopers. "Apache!"

Fly ran crazily into the darkness. He scrambled past the fire yelling, "Apaches! Apaches!" The civilians jumped together, holding each other instead of their guns. "Major! On the mountain! *Apache!*" His words were garbled. The major did not need to know what he had said—it was written on his face.

The wolf abruptly stood, revealing the muscled, lithe figure of White Horse. The animal skin was strapped tightly to his back and legs. Braced under a great, rounded rock were several logs. Running back from them was a heavy, rough plank of wood. It was positioned as a lever, the logs the fulcrum. White Horse laid his back under the wood lever. He strained with all his strength. Two shots sprayed against the rocks behind him. Stones splattered at his feet. Slowly, with the determination of the centuries, he started to move the lever. The wood creaked and moaned. The rock began to tremble. The warrior pitted all his might against the huge boulder. It began to move, inch by inch. Shots kicked up powdered stone around him. In one final lunge of energy, White Horse pushed his entire weight against the lever. The rock groaned, then began rolling toward the edge. Suddenly, it plummeted down over the side. Rocks cascaded, multiplied—right down upon the soldiers—a mammoth wave of sliding, hurtling stone and earth. The sounds intensified until nothing else could be heard. Only the roar of a landslide, building into the surging fury of an avalanche.

Chapter Seven

The power and volume of the moving earth inside the cave was greater than any sound they had ever heard before. The whole mountain shook. The horses stampeded. Some galloped frantically out through the mouth of the Caves and were immediately stoned to death. Others ran blindly around the cavernous room. The walls, the ceiling, the floor quaked violently. Men and women alike screamed, trying vainly to block out the deafening roar.

Outside, the lieutenant and the soldiers dropped their rifles. They looked up. Their necks stiffened as if pulled by strings. Their mouths fell open, but no cries or words came out. Their eyes grew wider. They stared in stunned awe as the mountain simply fell down upon them. First a heavy cloud of dust sprayed over them. They did not blink, but stared mutely skyward. For they were looking at Death. Then, in one massive wave, tons of split rocks and mounds of granite crushed them. Then they screamed. Some were gone immediately. The mountain continued to fall over them. They were quickly covered, as if they had never been there. As if the ledge, the overhang, and the cave had never existed. Skeleton Canyon had been given a new face.

The rumbling avalanche continued to pound like an angry fist against the mountain. Even inside, small rocks were being shaken loose from the ceiling of the Cave. They all moved back, stumbling over each other. Their mouths opened in terror, but no sound could be heard except for the raging mountain.

Finally the roar slowed. The captives continued to

scream, now able to hear their own panic. The rumble faded into a sigh. And then all was still. The men and women were suddenly so quiet that even the sound of their heart beats gave them a start. Then slowly, instinctively, they drew together, shaking, whimpering. They clutched each other.

The cavern was filled with swirling clouds. They coughed and choked. The major cautiously moved toward the entrance. The others followed in one trembling mass. The major looked in disbelief. A shudder of despair went over them all. The entrance had been sealed shut.

"Oh, Gawd!" Old Gabe moaned.

Baby Doe, Mrs. Ducks, and Eli Fly began to cry. Corporal Gatewood, Venable Brown, and the judge made a wild dash for the sealed entrance. They began desperately clawing at the tightly packed wall of rocks. They scratched at it like animals. Their hands and fingers became bloodied. Tears were streaming down their faces. They ranted at the impenetrable wall.

"Help us!" the judge cried out at the others. Barrett slumped on the ground. In his hand was his notebook. He clutched it like a child.

The major made his way to them. "It's no use. We're trapped—sealed in!"

"You wanted us to die from the start!" the judge screamed at him.

The major suddenly slapped him hard across the face. "Shut up, Tasker!" The judge only glared at the major, then began to tremble.

Sergeant Talbot broke out of his daze. He stumbled before him, waiting to be told what to do, too shaken to think of himself.

The major barked, "You men, stop that digging!" Then he and the sergeant began to pull the men away from the rocks.

"Got to dig out," Corporal Gatewood moaned over and over. He continued throwing rocks away from the wall. He remembered the months he had spent in the fort stockade for going A.W.O.L. They had made him tear down a small mountain, rock by rock, and move it over, thirty feet, by himself. That had been his punishment. And now, he was trapped again. He had begun to move another mountain.

"No use!" The sergeant tried again to pull the man back.

"Got to—" Gatewood screamed. "Got to get out." He struggled with the sergeant.

Talbot shouted down to him, "I'll tell you what to do, Gatewood, since you're on your knees. I'll tell you what to do—*pray*, you sonofabitch!"

The message had gotten through.

Gatewood dropped the rocks in his hands and slowly got off his knees. Everyone turned to Major Pilcher, their faces begging.

"That opening is hammered shut with a wall of rocks."

"Like a coffin!" Venable said bitterly.

"By Apaches," the judge added with finality.

Bull Whacker made a break for the remaining horses. He ran crazily into the wild-eyed herd. The animals moved away from him, as they had scattered from the bear. He grabbed the major's terrified horse and swung up. He spurred the animal. It reared in confusion, then bolted straight toward the huddled, whimpering women. The major sprinted after him. "What the hell you doing, Bull Whacker?"

"Ridin' out, that's what!" He lashed at the major with a riding quirt. The major grabbed it and wrestled the man off his horse. They struggled on the ground for a few moments. Finally, the major had him straddled like a horse.

"Easy man. Easy!" Bull Whacker squirmed like a hog-tied calf and then went limp. He turned his face to the floor and heaved convulsively. The major slowly got up, trying to catch his wind.

Mrs. Ducks started running around, hitting into the walls crying, "God! Help us! Please, help—" Her husband ran over to her. "Sarah!" She continued running blindly. He grabbed her.

"I don't want to die!" she whimpered. "Help us, please!"

He shook her. "Hush, before the Lord hears you and turns you to salt like Lot's wife!" She slowly slumped to the ground with her slack body in his arms. His head pressed against hers. Suddenly, everyone had become quiet.

"How many we got in here?" the major began counting. The sergeant counted with him.

"Twelve!" the sergeant blurted out. Then, Dull Knife appeared from one of the dark tunnels that led off from the cavern. "Thirteen. We still got our scout."

The major was not superstitious, but he did believe in bad luck. "Thirteen, " he mused. The significance of the number sunk into those around the room. No, they were not superstitious, just unlucky.

"What about those out there?" Barrett asked softly.

"Don't know,' the major answered, still stunned. "There may be more than a dozen bodies out there crushed under those rocks!"

Sergeant Talbot sat down. "And seven horses and five mules."

"For all we know, dead!"

Smoke swirled from out of what was moments before the mouth of the cave. Vultures had already alighted on rocks around the still settling avalanche. Their long, scrawny necks hung low, almost brushing the ground. Their eyes scanned the surface. There would be plenty for them to feast on. Suddenly, there was some movement in the rocks. The birds of prey scattered. Their shrill caws bounced eerily around the canyon.

The lieutenant was sunk into blackness, his mind splintered with pieces of words, sentences that ran through his head, "Get up, Sonny! Wesley!" He shook his head. Two arms, fat, female arms, reached down for him. The nightmare turned crazily in his head. More voices. "God ain't dead, Sonny, you're the man of the house now, boy!" Then he was standing over his mother's grave. The minister was talking, his mouth wide, but no words uttered forth. He felt sharp pain, even in his blackness. He had to break out. With great effort, he pulled open his eyes.

A great weight pressed down upon him. He began to panic and thrash about, but stopped when the pain knifed through his chest. He was wedged beneath a heap of rubble. He began to squirm. Inch by inch he wormed his way out of his rock tomb, breathing deep, bathed in sweat. Finally, he rested his head against something soft. He glanced down to see a lifeless arm sticking out from between some stones. The man shuddered and felt dazed, ill. Several of the soldiers moved. Scattered all around were torn, blood-soaked shirts, covering twisted human wrecks that would never move again.

Inside the cave, Baby Doe started whimpering. "All my cases, my clothes!" Her knees sagged to the floor.

Barrett mumbled weakly, "You got two suitcases right here, Baby Doe." His words brought her no comfort.

The major, his face drained, fumbled in his pockets for his pouch of tobacco. "God, all of them. Lieutenant Bernard, Oddie, Goddin, Yager, Hicks. . . ." He was shaking too much to roll a cigarette. The pouch dangled in his limp hands.

"Butterfield, Slack . . ." sergeant mumbled.

"And just by a twist of fate—by the blink of a cat's eye—almost, my friend, Mr. Eli Fly." Fly went to him. He clung to Barrett. The two men held each other.

"Poor Wesley," the major shook his head. "Under that uniform was a gutsy boy fighting to get out."

The others stared at him. Seeing him so shattered gave them cause to panic.

"I'm afraid, Joshua," Fly sobbed, "we're all going to die. . . ."

Outside, the lieutenant held his side, which throbbed with each deep breath. He could not feel anything broken, but his whole body felt like one massive bruise. Half-walking, half-clawing his way, he staggered over to one of the soldiers. Private Orley was curled in a heap. The lieutenant touched his shoulder softly. The soldier saw him, swallowed.

"Easy now, Orley." The lieutenant helped him sit. "You're alive, same as me."

Orley trembled. "The whole mountain tumbled down on us."

The lieutenant looked up to the spot where he had seen the wolf. "It didn't tumble, it was pushed." Then he painfully stood. "Come, give me a hand with Hicks and Goddin."

"The rest?" Orley did not move.

The lieutenant looked over the gaping wound of the mountain. "They're either crushed and broken," he nodded toward the mangled heap of flesh and bones, "as you can see, buried under a hundred tons of rocks, or alive and need us."

"What about them inside?"

"That's what we have to find out." Bernard reached for Orley's arm. "Now, put your arm over my shoulder."

The major started walking back and forth before them. "Now, we're not dead. And neither are the Apaches in here with us!" They were trying to read his thoughts. Major Pilcher kicked some dirt off his boots. "Now look!" He pointed suddenly. "If that's the only entrance, then how did that Indian on top get there?"

Old Gabe came to life. "*Sure!* If *he* got out, then there's a way. There *must* be!"

"It's not this way—it's *that!*" the major pointed excitedly off into the caves. "We'll just, all of us, have to go, if need be, clear out to Mexico—or Hell!" He had made a decision.

The others were taking all this in. Their faces were unsure, dubious, resentful, and afraid.

The major walked over to Fly. "Mr. Fly! You sure you saw only *one* Apache on that mountain?"

Fly nodded feebly, "Yes, sir."

"Good." The major continued thinking. He rubbed his thumb into the palm of his other hand as he walked. "Then, he's out and we only got three Apaches in here."

"Well, that does a lot of good," the judge said with sarcasm. "We're just as well dead."

"We still have guns, Tasker."

"We have them outnumbered," Venable perked up. "Don't forget that, Judge."

"Sure," Old Gabe smiled grimly running his thumb along the edge of his knife. "I'll settle for three more scalps at a hundred each." He grinned at the major. "You kill them and I'll sign my autograph on their heads."

The major stopped in front of Fly. "Mr. Fly, was the Apache on the mountain old, stocky, craggy-lookin'?"

Fly's voice quivered. "He was tall—and wiry."

The major looked oddly relieved. "Then it wasn't Geronimo."

"That sounds like it was White Horse," offered the sergeant. The poster of Geronimo at every fort was unmistakable.

Barrett's dazed eyes were strangely vacant. "How do you know White Horse won't come back in?" His knuckles had turned white from his unyielding grip around his notebook. He wound and unwound the frayed pages around his pen.

"I don't." The major looked at all their glazed eyes. "But if I know Apaches, my guess is Geronimo sent him on to rejoin the rest of their raiding party."

"Well, shoot!" the sergeant stood, his voice almost renewed. "That's three of them—and all of us. What are we afraid of? It's no worse than it was before!"

"The odds may be in our favor," the judge spoke wryly, "except now, we're trapped. As a gambling man, I'd just as soon bet on *them*. Any takers?"

"Aw, shut up, Tasker," Venable glared at him. He had lost too often at the hands of gambling men like the judge. After close to forty years of scratching the earth to dig up just enough for a grubstake now and then, Venable had come to learn to respect only one thing—callouses. He could tell by a man's hand if he could be trusted or not. The judge's hands were smooth, except for the telltale dealers' ridge on his thumb. Venable was not as worried as the rest. He had spent most of his life in tunnels, digging like a rat. Being holed up in these caves would be little different from his normal life. He lived like a rat or a mole. He would die like one, too.

"What are we going to do, Major?" Mrs. Ducks asked simply.

"Find the way out," he said without hesitation. "Through ten or eleven miles of caves!"

The prospect sat uneasily and harrowingly on all their faces, military and civilian alike.

Private Hicks' foot had been wedged between several jagged boulders. It was badly mangled. Hunks of skin were stuck on the sharp teeth of the stones. Words were beyond him. He shuddered as the lieutenant gingerly bandaged his foot with a torn piece of shirt.

Goddin was in better shape. He leaned against a rock and grimaced. "See that? My old, drunk Daddy was right; trust in God and keep away from work." He slid his hand into a crevice and wrestled out a mangled canteen. After taking a long drink, he said seriously, "Yeah, Orley, if I hadn't been sluffing off, aways from the Cave's mouth, why I would've been crushed like a caterpillar. . . ." His eyes became moist, his lips quivered as he realized just how close they had all come to death. Orley stared at him a moment, then looked away. Both were overcome with emotion.

"Orley, Goddin!" The lieutenant was making his way precariously over the huge piles of rocks, pointing. "There's some more moving—" He hobbled off. The two men struggled after him, up over the rocks.

"Except, Major," the judge said after wetting his convictions, "my judicious mind tells me there's a better choice right here—digging!"

"How in hell do you figure to burrow through a couple hundred feet of solid rock, man?"

"A couple hundred feet's better'n ten miles, Major." Gabe was sharpening his knife on a stone.

"We'll be lost if we go into them caves," Bull Whacker added. "We'll die for sure!"

The judge felt his back snapping as he stooped and picked up a large rock. Briefly staring at the major with defiance, he threw the rock heavily off. It rolled and crashed noisily down. "Gabe?" He panted from the effort. "Venable? Bull Whacker?" His forehead was running with sweat. "Come on, the sooner we start digging, the sooner we get out!" He reached for another stone, but leaned heavily against it to catch his breath.

"Now, Judge," Gabe came to him. "You're not used to heavy work. Maybe the major's right."

"He hasn't been right so far, has he? He's the one that got us in here!" The judge lifted another stone and threw it heavily down.

Bull Whacker looked at the judge with his one good eye. His glass eye never closed. Some people said he had the Evil Eye and they avoided him. He preferred it that way, ever since the day he had been left behind as dead by some good Christian, God-fearing people. The Apaches had taken his eye; his white compatriots had taken his faith in anyone except himself. Slowly he scanned the group, inwardly smiling at the unsettling effect his unblinking stare caused. His size, well over six feet, and his eye gave men a start and him an edge, which he needed as his head had never been right since he had lost that eye.

Often friendly Indians he had dealt with would come over just to stare at the eye that did not blink. It frightened them with its cold, staring look. They truly believed it to be a Spirit's eye and feared Bull Whacker as if he were some strange and powerful God. It had even spared his life once when he had been captured by hostile Blackfeet. His two pals had been killed and Bull Whacker was to have been next. But, the Blackfeet had been fascinated by the eye. They had crowded around him and asked if he was a God. If it really was an Evil Eye? Bull Whacker had said yes, and to prove it, to their amazement, he had taken the eye out and had held it aloft. They had backed off in fear. Then, quick as a flash, he had popped it back into his head. They had run from him as if he were the Great White Spirit himself, which they had offended into wrathful anger.

Bull Whacker, in reality, was slow-witted. Words did not come easy to him. Any learning he had had was lost to him now. He spoke slowly, his voice paced unevenly as he thought out loud. "If it was two hundred feet. . . ." They all looked at him. "And we all pitched in—why we could maybe do it in five, six weeks."

"Make it seven weeks." Venable stared at the glass eye with fascination.

Major Pilcher said with strained patience, "It'll take months!"

"Being a prospector, I say the major's right," Venable reflected in a professional voice.

The major pointed to the blocked entrance. "That wasn't a rock slide out there—it was an avalanche!" They all looked confused. No one moved. The judge sat disconsolately. He kicked down a few small stones.

"They're trapped in there—" the lieutenant stared into the impenetrable wall of rocks. "And we've got to get them out." He was kneeling on a pile, which he judged to be close to the entrance. Sitting and standing below him now were nine, still very shook up and tattered, soldiers.

"But, they got most of the supplies." Orley sat. He was hungry and scared.

"All we got is fresh air," Goddin snapped sarcastically. He knew what it meant to be caged. Andersonville Prison had held him for three bitter, long years. He had spent the duration of the Civil War fighting to survive in that black stink hole. He still could not decide if his battle in the confederate prison had been crueler than the war itself. Only one man out of ten had made it through Andersonville—he had been one of them. Sure, they were shook and beat up, but at least they were outside and alive.

"We've got to get them out, that's all there is to it, boys." The lieutenant had found a purpose, which made him forget his sore and beaten body. The others were still too depleted to do more than stare. "We're setting the camp back up first thing. Then, it's digging. In shifts. Night and day. All of us." He looked from face to face. They were troubled. He sensed that he had to give them drive and purpose.

"Why can't we blast 'em out with dynamite?" Orley asked.

"Our dynamite's soaken wet. Besides it would probably bring down the rest of the mountain." He felt their uneasiness. He was not sure how to rally them. Nothing at the point had prepared him for this. The spit and polish of the army regimen were useless now. He tried to control his voice, tried to hide the gut depression that was creeping over him like sand on a desert floor.

Goddin looked around at the arms and legs that jutted out from between rocks. "What about the dead?"

For a long moment no one said anything. They glanced around at the pieces of mangled bodies. Their gaze did not stay too long on any one horror. The sight was too cruel.

"We'll bury what the mountain didn't." From the lieutenant's tone, it was clear he felt it was better for them to be told what to do than to let them think on what had happened.

"What about the Apache wolf?" Orley peered up along the rocky cliff. "He's probably still up there."

"We'll keep a guard posted all the time."

"That's one damn animal I'd like to skin alive."

"You may get the chance, Hicks." The lieutenant started taking off his shirt. "Come on, boys! We dig!" He wrapped the shirt tightly around his chest. It eased the pain somewhat. "It's going to be a long haul."

"Months . . ." Orley mumbled dimly, depressed.

"One rock at a time." Hicks bent down, picked up a large stone. Lugging rocks was second nature to him. He had spent most of his boyhood clearing his father's barren land in Illinois. People said his father's farm was the very bowels of hell. Nothing ever grew on it except rocks and weeds. When other folks were harvesting their crops, his family was still clearing rocks. In fact, when he had left home, his old man had been in the field wrestling with a boulder that had snagged the plow. With a resigned heave, Hicks hurled the stone.

"They built the Pyramids that way, we can open up a mountain," the lieutenant said lifting away. "We're coming, Major!"

"I joined the cavalry to ride horses," Orley said. "I could've done this in any damn jail!" His rock tumbled and bounced to the canyon floor.

Those inside had broken into three groups. The major, the sergeant, Corporal Gatewood, and Dull Knife were packed and ready to move out. In the middle, standing uneasily were Barrett, Venable, Old Gabe, Mr. and Mrs. Ducks, and Baby Doe. Standing below the judge indecisively, was Bull Whacker. Eli Fly sat by himself quietly. He was surrounded by his equipment. He was agitated, torn, and hesitant.

The judge climbed higher onto the pile then whirled around and stared them all down. "Who's staying with me?" No one moved. "I'm getting out the way I came in!"

"How's that, Judge?" Gabe shouted up to him, "Drunk?"

"No, alive!" With each rock he moved, another took its place. Undaunted, he kept up his futile work.

The major turned to those in the middle: "Mr. Ducks—are you and your missus coming with me?"

One lens of Sidney Ducks' spectacles was cracked. "Those Apaches in there know these caves like the backs of their hands." Despite his farmer's build, he had a great inner strength—like his wife, Sarah. While hers was derived from her God, his was wrested entirely from his need for her. His father had signed a contract when they both had been one month old—on neighboring farms. At fourteen they had wed. The years had filtered down, through trial and tribulation, almost thirty of them, and still his feeling for her grew. Few knew it, but they had never, not for one day, since they had taken their vows been apart. They were truly inseparable. Even while working in the fields, he had always yearned for her back in the house. A separation of a few miles sent a pain of longing to his heart. She felt the same. It was as if they were one. He seldom spoke of it; there was no need to. Now, thanks be, to the providence of God, even in their danger, they were at least together.

"They'll be laying for us at every turn," Venable said. He could not decide which of the two men—the major or the judge—was the bigger fool.

"I already lost one eye to them." Bull Whacker tapped on his fake eye. "See this one, it's glass. It don't blink." As if they didn't know. He shook his head. "No thanks. I know Apaches. I'm staying put!"

"They can see in the dark like cats," old Gabe yammered.

"If we move, we're dead," Bull Whacker prophesied.

The major spit. "If you stay, you're dead. Just believe me—I can do anything any Apache can."

"You can," Mr. Ducks said dryly, "but can we?"

"With two women tagging along?" Baby Doe slumped on two suitcases.

79

"You forget . . ." the sergeant piped up, "we got Dull Knife!"

The major affirmed trying to reassure them. "He's as sure-footed as a goat, got toes like nails, and a nose that can smell an Indian a mile off."

"Gabe said suspiciously, "How can we trust him?"

"He's one of us," said Sergeant Talbot. "He's just like any soldier."

"What do we have to eat?" Gabe wanted to know.

"We're low," Corporal Gatewood answered evasively, "but we got enough to last."

"If we have to, we'll eat what the Apaches eat."

Gatewood looked at the major. "Bats?"

"And if need be, mules!"

"And horsemeat?"

The major eyed Venable slowly. "Maybe. But nobody's touchin' my gray." He swung up on the animal. "Follow or stay—do as you damn well like!"

Old Gabe quickly threw his pack and strings of scalps over his shoulder. "Well, if worse come to worse, we can always eat our boots. I did once in winter." In truth, he had. He had boiled the leather in a broth for hours, beat it to a pulp, rolled it up into little balls—and slowly, masticated it to digestible bits. It certainly had stopped the yowling in his stomach.

The major turned his horse and began to move off. Bull Whacker went after him, running in front of the gray and stopped it. "I'm sorry, Major. I'd like to go with you, I swear. But, we been wandering for five weeks with no stop. I'd just as soon stay put and chance it here with the judge." The cavalry had never dealt him a fair hand, but then, neither had the judge. Trust in what you can see was his belief and he was sticking to it. He knew what was here, but out there in the dark? Only a fool would follow the major. Bull Whacker shuffled back to join the judge, even his glass eye looking baleful.

"That's your decision, boys," the major shouted back. "We rationed out what food and water we could.

If anybody else wants to stay and dig, I'm not stopping you. It's on your *own* bloody heads. As God is my witness, I warned you!" He moved off again. The sergeant, Corporal Gatewood, and Dull Knife, all leading pack mules, strayed after him. Talbot, holding one burning torch, followed a wide path of light which descended from a great hole high over them in the rock ceiling.

A desperate rush went through the group. They began to gather up their belongings. One at a time, they broke away. Baby Doe lifted her bags. Dragging, kicking and pulling them, she started off after the major. Venable furiously tied his tools onto his mule, which was already loaded with packs of wood, as well as pickaxes, shovels, ropes, and pans—and went clanging after the major.

Barrett was slowly trailing the others. He carried nothing but his notes. He was still oddly subdued and passive. His story was with the major. Fly stopped him.

"I can't, Joshua," he said, very emotional. "I can't leave my life's work. All my equipment. You understand?" There was no question in Fly's mind. To be without his equipment would be like being without blood. He would be sapped, useless, without his buffer against the world. Small in stature, he had acclimated to a tall world. His pictures were his strength, his voice. He could not leave them behind.

Barrett touched his shoulder. "Eli, it's your decision: If you feel you must, stay." He hesitated and then began to walk away. "We'll make it! We'll work together again, you'll see. Good luck!"

Fly's eyes were brimming. "Get your story, Joshua! Remember, it's half mine, too! God bless the *St. Louis Dispatch* and the president of the United States!"

Barrett went, trailing reluctantly, obviously still far from convinced.

Several soldiers and the lieutenant, all stripped to the waist and sweating, lifted and threw. Their backs ached so much that they did not straighten up to hurl. They stayed bent as they lifted and threw. They did not stop or complain. A rough campsite had been set up. A small fire was going. Some rabbits were hung on stakes, half skinned to dry in the sun. Two guards, rifles ready, patrolled the camp. Below them, just removed from sight, were seven, rough wood crosses over piles of fresh earth. It was better that they were not reminded. The men worked easier now that the dead had been buried.

Ely Fly drifted back to the judge, and the giant Bull Whacker. They all stared off after the single torch light flickering in the distance until it disappeared. No one spoke. The weight of indecision pressed too heavily. No one moved. Long minutes crept by as they continued to stare out at nothing.

Then the judge broke the spell. His wrists cracked as he hoisted up a rock. His legs trembled. The rock slammed against stone below. The sound echoed in the empty chamber.

Fly wandered back to his equipment. He mindlessly began fidgeting with a tripod. He could not take his eyes off the engulfing black. He could not stop his thoughts. Worry and dread slipped over him like a shroud.

"We don't need you to take pictures, Fly." The judge grunted as he raised another stone, "Puny as you are, you got to lift rock—or you don't eat!"

"Don't worry. I'm stronger than I look. It's the little men that built the world, Judge Tasker!" To prove it, half-killing himself, he settled over a huge rock. Straining with all his strength, he brought it off the ground. It rolled off the pile. He straightened up and smiled. Then with trembling arms, Fly reached for another. . . .

The major had slowed down to let the others catch up. They looked like wagonless gypsies. Everyone carried their own load; the mules, wood. Without fire they would be lost. Their steps were already faltering. Their eyes were masked in misgiving and fear. Only Venable showed little sign of fatigue or hardship. The major rode back to him.

"You can carry more than that, Venable!"

Venable had only one canteen draped across his chest. "That's what my mule's for!"

The major pulled off one of Venable's rolls from the overloaded mule. "He's got his job, this is yours!" He thrust the roll over Venable's shoulder and rode on ahead.

"You got to take all those scalps, Gabe?" The major pulled up next to him.

"Scalps? That's my payday!" The major shook his head at their foolishness. Their lives depended on their strength, yet they would wear themselves out for their possessions.

Baby Doe was having a hard time with her two cases. Barrett tried to help her with one hand.

"I can handle it, Mr. Barrett," she resisted.

"Why kill yourself? I can carry one."

"Thanks, but I carry my own in this world!" She moved on stubbornly.

At the end of the line, Mrs. Ducks slowed down. She hesitated, then sat on a rock. Her husband came back to her. He took her hand, "Come on, Sarah."

"You go on a bit, Mr. Ducks. I just want a quick prayer—alone with my God."

"All right, Sarah. But don't tarry."

"I'll be right along," she called after him. Then, she knelt and looked heavenward. "Dear God," she looked peacefully into the darkness around her, "in your name, and your will, I'm resigned, humbly and meekly. Watch over me—us—but, if you want my life, it be yours. Amen." Slowly, she got to her feet and followed after the others. As she walked, she softly sang a hymn: "I come to the garden a-lone. A voice, I heard. Was none other than His. *And* He walks with me. And He *talks* with me, and His voice, it is my own. . . ."

As she sang, her head held firm, her eyes were fixed straight ahead. Suddenly, a figure moved out on catlike feet from the darkness. A leather lariat swung loosely in hands. It suddenly whirled around her throat. It tightened before she could cry out. The figure jerked her down to the hard, stone ground. She did not even try to fight. They say the moment of death is the moment of truth. It is not, it is the moment just before that. How much can one cram into that precise moment? Curiously, she was swept back to her mother's garden. The old woman was reaching out and handing her a rose. Merely that and nothing more. For one fraction of a second, Sarah was a tall, spindly, bright girl and then the memory was twisted off. Forever. All memory and time. There was a short, crisp movement, then a sigh. Then, deathly silence.

Chapter Eight

The grottos, chasms and shafts of the caves filled with soft, whispered calling. A mixture of voices echoed in the hollow chambers. "Sarah, Mrs. Ducks, Sarah, darling." Their voices overlapped. The words reverberated and redoubled. Torch lights flickered against the damp walls. Unearthly shadows climbed the rocks and disappeared. Then one by one, the voices died and lilted away, like dry, drifting leaves. The caverns once more were silent.

It was hot. The party was soaked and sweating. Some were coughing and gagging. They sat weakly, all strung out, along a large pool. The steaming, hot water swirled up between rock crevices. Clouds of vapor hung over the pool and enveloped them.

Sidney Ducks paced, nervously chewing his lips, his face contorted. His emotions had gotten the better of him. The major watched him, withdrawn. Baby Doe sobbed silently.

"Another hour! Just one!" He wrung his hands and whimpered. "Please!" He made a pained noise. "Have a heart! One more hour!" He begged, "Major, in the name of Christ!"

The major beseeched him with his eyes to understand. "I'm sorry, Mr. Ducks." He touched the old man. "We already spent six hours searching for her!"

"Is *one* more so much to ask?" He was confused, staring accusingly at them all.

"We done the best we could," Sergeant Talbot muttered. "Searched high and low." God knows, the sergeant thought, we tried, as he remembered the time his brother drowned, and he had searched the muddy waters for half a day until he knew that the great fist under the dark had dragged his brother away forever.

"I must've called her name a thousand times," Venable interjected.

"Then where *is* she?" Sidney Ducks collapsed to his knees. "Where's my Sarah?" He shuddered. They were frightened. There was nothing they could do.

"Lost," Barrett mumbled weakly.

"Just like the rest of us." In frustration, Venable hurled a rock at the black that surrounded them. "Lost and out of luck!" He whirled around and faced the major. "Aren't we, Major?"

"Shut up, Venable—nobody's lost!"

"Not yet, I says." He muttered to himself. He spat a brown glob of tobacco into the pool.

Old Gabe dropped his scalps on the ground. "There's nothin' back there, Mr. Ducks. No sign of her or Apaches. My feet are falling off from searching."

"You saw for yourself, Mr. Ducks," the major crouched down next to him. "We found nothing except holes. Black, bottomless holes. We looked, Mr. Ducks—*you* looked." He patted the farmer on the knee. "She wasn't there," he said, trying to be convincing.

"She must've fell down one of them holes." The sergeant uttered. "I almost fell down one myself."

Too much had happened too fast. Baby Doe had never been a crier, but since her husband had died and left her penniless, her stamina had cracked. She thought she had gotten control of herself when she left Denver, the scene of her most ungracious downfall. The debilitating sense of helplessness had overwhelmed her when the stagecoach had been plundered by the Apaches. The last month had been a half-remembered nightmare. All she knew was that she was being swept along, against her will, and she had no power to stop it.

Sidney Ducks looked at them incredulously. "You mean—she just fell?" He shook his head. "Down and down and down?" He looked faint. "But to *where?*"

"Maybe China, Sid," Venable said. They all gave him a stare. "God only knows!" he added lamely.

The major was not good at giving comfort. "If she has, she's buried in the middle of the earth."

"Her body all broke up?" Ducks rose to his feet. "We got to get her! Maybe she's still alive!" He started to go. "She's out there, hurt and bleeding, calling my name!"

The major came after him, put his arm around the trembling man. "Listen, Mr. Ducks, if she fell down one of those holes, she's surely dead. Nobody could ever climb out, you *must* see that—"

"She could've gone back to the others, couldn't she?"

"Doubt that, Mr. Ducks," the sergeant said. "Not even I could find my way back there now." He looked away from the pleading man's eyes.

"It's not right, it's not fair!" He pulled away. "She didn't want to go down into the bowels of the earth," he broke down, "she wanted to go up to Heaven and wait for me. She told me!" He sunk to the stone. "Now, she fell clean through to Hell. She didn't deserve to!" His eyes were twisted, almost mad. "Look about, friends— see the steam—the smoke? The air be putrid and stagnant. It's sulphur. *Smell* it!" The major tried to stop him, but he waved him away. "It's the Devil's smoke! It stinks! It's given us cramps. Death cramps! It'll kill us all!" They looked at him with their own alarm. "Feel this heat? We're all in *Hell!* We're bein' punished for our sins! We're dead and in Hell! We're all dead, *dead!*" Sobbing desperately, he dropped to his knees again and beat his head on the stone.

They worked much slower now, almost in a daze. Bull Whacker stopped. He leaned against a rock, his great strength depleted. He squinted up curiously, following a wide shaft of light. His neck creaked, as he strained to see the source. High above them was the large crack in the stone ceiling of the Cave. It was hundreds of feet away. From that distance it looked about the size of his hand.

"Stop dawdling, Bull Whacker!" The judge pushed him roughly. Bull Whacker stumbled, scraping his legs on the rough stone. He slowly picked up another rock. He held it for a moment looking at the judge. Then putting aside the thought of crushing open his skull, he continued working with pained movements. They saw nothing but the granite in front of them.

Just for a second, the shaft of light was broken. No one noticed. If they had, they would have known that more than the judge was watching their labors. For now, high above them, two cold, black, human eyes were glaring down. White Horse in his wolf skin surveyed the forlorn group.

The judge slumped down. His lips were cracked from the constant sweat which bathed his face. His chest constricted as he gasped for breath. He swore to himself that he would never work like this again. "We're almost out of whiskey." He sounded desperate at the thought. He turned on Fly. "I think you been stealing it, Fly."

Fly looked at him and shook his head. "I don't drink." He could barely speak. The exertion made his lungs feel close to bursting. He stooped to move another stone, coughed, farted secretly, and sat.

"We still got some tiswin," Bull Whacker dropped a hunk of limestone with a clattering bang. "I stole it from Dull Knife. Y'ever try drinking that poison?"

"Nah. But it might come to that." He still eyed Fly suspiciously.

"Well, don't." Bull Whacker kicked some gravel down with his feet. "It would choke a buffalo. I heard they even boils live frogs in it." Sardonically, he added, "I'd drink my own piss, before I'd drink that poison."

Fly wrestled with another rock. It would not move. Bracing with his foot, he jerked it out. He cursed under his breath, "Every time I pull out one rock—another comes down to take up the space it occupied!"

"Well," the judge commented, "you just discovered the secret of the world. . . ."

The soldiers worked in two lines, passing down the rubble along them. They had barely made a dent. It seemed that with every rock removed, two or three took its place. There had to be a better way. Wesley cursed himself for not having paid more attention to his engineering course at the Point. He had no experience to draw from, having never done manual labor in his life. Like a child furrowing in a sand pile, he could only hope that sheer stubbornness would clear the way. He kept fighting back the waves of despair that broke somewhere off beyond him. His heart was beginning to sink at the sheer magnitude of the task he had set before him. But life was at stake. Perhaps, even his own.

The major had stopped. Ahead of them, in the dark passageway, was something foreign to the cave. The light from their torches made it glow like the Devil's teeth.

"What in hell is that?" The sergeant warily moved forward with his smoking torch extended.

The major walked ahead, leading his horse. He knelt down for a closer look. "Horse bones, plucked clean!" The others bunched up behind them.

"Well, at least that explains what the Apaches have been living on." The major kicked the pile of bones.

"And scalps." Corporal Gatewood gingerly touched one with his foot, then picked it up with the end of his rifle. "White scalps." He waved it around for all to see.

"How you know they wasn't black?" Old Gabe stared down at the mound of shriveled skin and hair.

"Because they got gold teeth. My people can't afford 'em!" Gatewood snapped sarcastically. Then he flung the scalp into the dark.

"Hey, mind them scalps!" Gabe rushed over. He started picking them up and hanging them on his belt.

The left side of the sergeant's face began twitching. He pulled at his cheeks to stop the nervous tick, but his awareness of it only increased its spasmodic pace. It had been a good ten years since his face had acted up like that. Same sort of thing brought it on, too—being locked up. Stifle, the doctors called it, stemming from childhood. He never could remember what that was, but he sure did not like having it. It made people think a man wasn't right in the head, made them look at him funny. Knowing he had it kept him out of trouble. A jail was no place for a man with a stifle on him, and for that matter, neither were these caves.

As a kid, for punishment, he had been locked in a closet. Later just his room. One day, to punish his mother he had locked himself in an old wooden trunk but could not get out. It had been like a coffin. He shouted all day until they had finally heard him. In the darkness of the trunk he had imagined he was dead. It was a feeling the sergeant would never forget.

"Want to play a little stud poker for your horse, Major?" Venable asked.

"You may be half kidding, Venable," the major said as he remounted, "but there isn't enough money in the world to buy this animal. Me and Dynamite been raised in the cavalry. He's eleven years old. Be too tough to eat, anyways. But he can still run. He'll turn on a quarter and give you fifteen cents change."

Venable patted the gray's back. There was the edge of a sly threat in his voice. "Well, I hope no starving body steals that beautiful animal in the middle of the night."

"The man that steals my horse owes me his life." The major spoke, his warning clear.

"I may be just an old saddle-sore scalper," Gabe mumbled, "but, I could eat a whole horse including the saddle."

"It's not starvation that'll do you in, friend. There could be your own murderer behind any one of those rocks out there." With that the major moved on.

Was it any different in life? Barrett thought to himself. Down any dark street, behind any pole or tree our own murderer lurked? It was an era of the killer, the enemy was oneself. We were our own killers. He had forced himself into a dangerous situation testing something in himself. Well this was the real test. The unknown was not the unknowable; it was not something out there, but something in our minds.

Their packs were lighter now. It made the going easier. But their stomachs were beginning to take a beating.

They moved on following, always following, the major. Fear pushed them on. Fear of the dark, of Apaches.

"Well, Major, which way is it?" The sergeant pointed his torch around. The room before them was like a natural carriage house, with trails and tunnels leading off in many directions.

"That way!" He pointed to a dripping black hole to their left.

"Why?"

Lowering his voice, he said, "I got a feeling we've been circling right too much."

The sergeant whispered as he limped, crept, along the tunnel. "I don't get it for dust." His boots were made for riding, not walking. "Why don't the Apaches try and pick us off, Major?"

"Like Mrs. Ducks?" he asked grimly.

The sergeant stared at him. "You said she fell in a hole?"

"I know what I said." He slowed up his horse. "A hole doesn't leave neck burns, does it?"

The sides of the tunnel were getting narrower and lower. At first it had barely been noticeable. But now the animals were scraping their heads against the ceiling. The major's horse was snorting and trying to back up. He tried to lead the animal on, but the horse could see what the major was not able. He cursed the horse and dragged it forward. He struggled a few dozen feet more and came right up against a dead-end. He looked worn and disgusted, feeling the way he looked.

"Hold it!" Sergeant Talbot yelled back to the rest of the party. They all stopped, grateful for the break. They propped themselves up against the slick, cold walls.

"We have to go back to where we were," the major called back, "and try one of the other tunnels."

"What about the horses—how do you suggest we turn them around?" a voice called from behind.

"We pull them out by their assholes!"

"You try backing up a mule, Major?" Gabe yelled.

Venable squeezed past the others. He blew up. "We wasted *two* hours comin' this way!"

"I can't see through rock, Mr. Brown." The major was trying to keep his temper. "I made a mistake. Haven't you ever?"

"Yeah," he glowered, "in joining up with the Fourth Cavalry!"

The walls were full of colorful minerals in beautiful splashes. No one noticed. They only stared glumly at the feet of the person ahead of them. Venable had thrown his pack over the mule he led. The animal slumped under the weight. The rope in Venable's hand kept its head up, otherwise it would have dragged to a halt.

"I can't go on. . . ." Baby Doe dropped her cases. Her hands were throbbing, blistered, and red. She could not feel her feet anymore. They were numb from the constant wet. No one stopped for her. She stared unbelieving as the torch lights rounded a corner and began to fade. Quickly wiping her nose on her skirt, she began dragging her cases after them.

The ledge was barely three feet wide. The major had crossed it already. He sat on his horse, below, watching the rest inch along it. It had taken better than three hours to get up and over. There had been no choice. It had been either the ledge or a jump over a six-foot chasm. They could not have taken the risk, although a few had argued for the leap. Perception in the Caves was distorted. He would have guessed no more than an hour to get over the ledge. Perhaps a few weeks ago he could have made it easy. But now each step was a bad experience. A slip or stumble, excruciating.

Barrett was the first down. His feet were bruised, and probably bleeding. He did not want to look. Somewhere along the way, he had lost his hat and tie and air of respectability.

"I'm sick. We haven't eaten today, Major." He slumped down and buried his head in his hands.

"Thanks for reminding me. I'll speak to Corporal Gatewood about it, Mr. Barrett." He moved away from him. He could not stand whimpering, even from a woman.

Barrett stumbled up. He grabbed the major's coat. "My pack's empty! Stop kidding me, Major. If we don't have any more food, just tell us, goddammit, *tell us!*"

"You're cracking up, Joshua."

"I got to have food!"

"You're getting bug-eyed. Pull yourself together, man!"

"When are we going to eat?"

"Soon, I promise you."

"When?"

The major jerked him up. "Think of your story, man! Think of the *St. Louis Star Dispatch!*" His voice had a caustic edge in it.

Barrett stared at him dumbly, "I can't."

As they waited for the others to catch up, Barrett idly took out his notebook. He stared at the blank pages. He did not have the strength to write. But he did. He wrote sentences, disjointed, broken, bits and pieces of his diffused thoughts, his reeling brain. Confused outpourings of verse:

> *If a man makes way, he will find no sound,*
> *But the sea wind's restless night and day. . . .*

And from John Donne:

> *No man is an Island . . .*
> *Each man's death diminishes me—*
> *I'll tell thee for whom the bells toll,*
> *They toll for thee, thee, thee. . . .*

The major became concerned as he watched Baby Doe struggle precariously over the ledge. She was almost across. Her hair was hanging in her face like a wild woman's. Her cases made her lopsided. She leaned dangerously over the side. He scrambled up the rocky incline. His legs ached. His joints were stiff. She gratefully accepted his hands.

"You'd be better off if you left them behind."

"I'd just as soon stay behind with them, Major." She eyed him with childlike suspicion.

"Let me take one—" He reached out for it. She clutched it closer to her chest.

"You said each one of us got to carry their own load. I'm not going to have nobody say I can't carry mine."

"Nobody'll say anything."

She began to soften, her toughness giving way to vulnerability. They walked. "We are getting out, aren't we, Major?" She smiled wanly, the female in her coming out at his presence.

"Sure we are. With luck." He avoided her eyes, as he carried one of the bags.

She asked again, "Promise?"

The major nodded. "Word of honor."

"What happens then, I mean, for you, after we get out?"

"Same as usual," he said without lament or hesitation.

She looked somewhat disappointed and surprised. "After all that's happened, you're going to pick up the same as before?"

He shrugged.

"Well, there must be better ways to earn a living

than being shot at by Indians!"

"What did you have in mind?" He stopped to let her rest, as she was breathing hard.

She thought for a moment. "Prospecting."

"Nah, that's only for fools," he fumbled. "Of course I didn't mean your late husband."

"He was the biggest fool of all."

"Put the shoe on the other foot. What are you going to do with the rest of your life?"

"Same as I done with the first!" She smiled. "Turn me upside down, swing me by the tail—like a cat—I land on my feet! I always go where I'm kicked. I've always been fate's fool."

He hesitated, "You got people to look after you?"

"I'm no schoolgirl, Major. I've been my only friend for more years than I'd like to admit. You got family?"

"Me? One sister left. Back in Kentucky. My kid brother got himself killed in the War. His commanding officer wrote me a letter." He offered his arm, as they traversed a gap in the ledge. "One day I had a brother, next a letter."

"That's life in the army, isn't it?"

"Ever thought of trying Tucson?" he asked shyly, avoiding her eyes.

"Not yet. What did you have in mind, Major?"

"Always like people I like to like what I do."

"Oh?"

"Folks coming in every day like cockroaches after bacon."

"You don't say," she whistled, impressed for his benefit.

He flushed slightly. "I'd be glad to show you around. Could even help you get settled."

She rolled the thought around inside of her head. Taking his arm, she asked, "What's your Christian name, anyhow?"

"Name's Emmett."

"Emmett," she said softly, almost seductively, but was too tired to put on airs. "And call me Baby Doe, for

God's sake!" There was pleading in her voice.

He helped her down the last part of the ledge. "Rest, Baby Doe. I'll tend to this." He hoisted her bag onto one shoulder and moved on. She slumped on a rock, watched him go. A wicked thought grew in her mind, like a grain of sand in an oyster shell.

She got up and started to follow, softly humming, "Here Comes the Bride. . . ." One lived in hope, or it was better to be buried. Hope was the name of the game. She smiled. She was a natural born schemer. Her mind was a chess board of moves. She could win as long as the opponent was a man. Men were grist for her mill. She whistled, half-amused at the ridiculous idea of it all. "Elizabeth," she chided herself, "you'd fall in love with a toad, if you got stuck in a pond."

It was better not to rest too long. Each time they sat it became harder to get up. If they stopped only to sleep and eat, they would be out all the faster. With this in mind, they did not complain, although their bodies screamed for relief. They straggled in a long line behind the major. As long as they could see his torch, they would not be lost.

The sergeant whispered to the major, "They could push lead at us from every corner." He spoke rapidly like a man with a fever. "They got the hardware. They could fill us with lead plums."

"That's not the game they're playing." The major was hoarse. His throat burned from the water they had been drinking. "They're waiting us out—waiting till we're weaker than pups." He coughed. His mouth was bitter and sore. "Then out of the dark— A knife, a rock, a leather thong around the throat?"

The sergeant drew his pistol. "If I could see them, I'd fill them so full of holes they couldn't float in brine." He waved his gun crazily, his face twitching, out of control.

The major hissed sharply. "Your brain's getting addled!" The sergeant snapped out of it. He became silent.

Two times in his life he had almost met his Maker.

He wondered—third time lucky? He had a morbid fear of his own death. Not just from the army, but from before. His whole family had been unlucky. His mother died of the typhoid when he was ten. He had watched her go. Then, his father had been struck by lightning. His sister had passed on in childbirth, his brother had drowned, so it went. He had witnessed every one. . . . The sad expression on Talbot's face cracked. He looked at the major with troubled eyes. "Hey, Major, give it to me straight. Are we lost?"

"Lost? You ask me if we're lost?" His tone was level, unemotional. "Yeah, we're lost. Hopelessly!"

It was a tiny alcove, like a chapel. A narrow split in the ceiling let in a sliver of light. There was no sound, not even the dripping of water. Sidney Ducks sat wrapped in a bundle of clothes and blankets. No one had noticed when he had stopped. He had watched them vanish. Not one head had turned to look for him. He absentmindedly reached for his pack. Not feeling it, he twisted his head around, trying to see it. Then, he remembered. He had dropped it somewhere back there. No mind, it didn't matter. He was beyond hunger. He waited patiently, as he had always done for Sarah. "She'll be by." He noticed something at his feet. He bent down. It was a half-eaten piece of hardtack. It must have fallen out of one of his pockets. More out of habit than anything else, he munched on it. It had no flavor. He could not taste anyway. "It's cool here—nice," he mumbled as he studied the rock formations. "I'm not going one step more." He nodded, letting the dark come to him. "I'm waiting for Sarah— she'll be by—I can wait." He coughed weakly, pathetically. He had become cold. From somewhere in the darkness of his mind, a light opened. A musical instrument strummed. What was it? Something from the distant past? Yes. That old zither Sarah had brought with her when they had married—where was it anyway? The sound called to him. . . .

Chapter Nine

Bull Whacker poured water over coffee grounds. The liquid barely discolored. They had been using the same grounds for days. Their coffee was gone except for the sludge at the bottom of the pot. Fly lay sprawled out on the pile of rocks, resting where he had worked. He had been too tired to even eat.

The men chewed the jerky slowly. The longer they ate, the longer they could stay away from their unrelenting task. No one spoke. Their tempers were growing shorter. The fewer words, the fewer fights. There was not the time or the energy for arguing.

Suddenly, the sound of the thud of rock on rock came into the Caves. They all looked up. Fly stirred from his sleep. The judge jumped up.

"You hear! They're out there!" He kicked Fly. "They're alive!" Fly looked at him in an exhausted daze. "They're digging in!" Then the judge's words sunk in. He scrambled to his knees.

Bull Whacker threw himself on the wall of rocks. He pressed his ear against them. "Listen!" They all became quiet. Each strained to hear. Their eyes danced back and forth. A heavy thud crept into the cave.

"We got to answer them!" Bull shouted. "Let 'em know we're in here!"

Fly scampered to his feet. "Here, I'll show you!" He picked up a rock as large as he could manage and dropped it. They all held their breaths.

"Hear that!" Lieutenant Bernard shouted. "They're in there! They know we're here!"

98

The judge pushed Fly away. "Stay back! Look out!" With all his might, his arms pulled up a boulder as large as his chest. He strained, his face flushed dangerously red. Then he flung it.

The soldiers were all kneeling over the sealed entrance. They heard the dim, distant thud.

Orley beamed.

Goddin slapped Hicks on the back. The soldiers jostled each other.

"They're alive!" The lieutenant stared into the mountain. "Thank God!" Wiping his eyes on his arm, he grinned at all the men. Then, he picked up yet another rock and threw it—heavily down to the floor of the canyon.

The troopers worked all day and into the night. The canyon lay uncomfortably and eerily under a cold blanket. The torch lights smoked black and wavered in the wind. Their backs, arms, and legs were twisted in knots. But their pace did not slow. They paused to rest only when their long shifts had ended.

Inside, there were no shifts. There was neither the food, nor the strength to keep going for more than a few hours at a time. They all sat around a small fire, listening to the soft, faraway thuds of the cavalry working outside. The sounds comforted them; soon they would be free. It was just a matter of time.

Mr. Fly was huddled and shivering in a blanket. He had dragged all his equipment near the fire. The exertion had taken a lot out of him, but he felt safer with it close to him. "Nice to know they're working all night through."

The judge stared at him hostilely out of the corner of his eye. "More than we can say for you, you pathetic little worm." He guzzled down a mouthful of tiswin. The taste almost choked him. The judge's head reeled from it. The high came too fast and was too hard. He, in fact, felt like he had been poisoned, but that did not stop him from drinking more of it.

"What'd you stay behind for anyways?" Bull Whacker asked Fly. One gulp of the tiswin had left him with a sore stomach and a nasty head. Even the noise from outside did not soothe him.

"My equipment." Fly limply waved his arm at the battered cases around him. "All this. Tripods, film packs, the latest cameras." He smiled nervously.

Bull Whacker kicked the box on which he sat. "What have you got in this box, Fly—food?"

"No, sir," Fly answered. "If I had, I would've shared it." They all looked at him skeptically. "It's negatives. Six months work." He looked at them with open, honest eyes. His head nodded rapidly to reaffirm what he had said. "I'd show you tomorrow, but the light hurts them." The men gazed back into the fire. Fly straightened up, cleared his throat. "I'm a famous photographer, gents." They looked at him again, not very impressed. "Ask Mr. Barrett."

"You go ask him." The judge jerked his head toward the dark. "He's out there—with that damn fool major and three killer Apaches."

The judge drank again, the brown liquid spilling over his swollen lips.

"What's so famous about you, Squirt?"

"I've been published in every big newspaper and magazine in the land. Done two presidents, seven generals. Lots of famous New York stage actresses, too!"

"Naked?" Bull Whacker squinted at him.

"Oh, no!"

The judge roared. "That's a good one. This little pisser couldn't hump a snake if you held its head!" Fly reddened.

"Bet he's one of them fairy fellas!" Bull Whacker squeaked his voice up high, "Aren't you, Fly Speck?" He slapped Fly's back, almost knocking him to the ground. The judge punched Fly's arm and kicked his legs. Fly tried to get up. Then, a cold fear crawled through him as he looked at his companions. Their filthy, brawling faces were barely human. Their raucous gaffs seemed more like hyenas' yowls. For the first time, he felt more frightened of them than of the Caves.

For relief from his agony, Fly's mind became a cinema of his past—focusing and refocusing on his many moments of glory, his moments of triumph. His mind's eye snapped visions to warm the black present. He smiled as he reran the dim negatives of his memory. His dreams flooded his head, day and night, all tumbling together. Somewhere in their confusion, the little speck of candle flame called life, he knew, must not be allowed to go out. There was so much more to do. So much more to photograph. The mountains of India? The mysterious East? The Dead Sea? The pure blue waters of the Mediterranean? All that, and more.

"Have a drink, Tiny." The judge pulled Fly back down. He shoved his canteen into Fly's hands, his foul breath enveloping the little photographer's face. Fly took it and stared at it dumbly. Just as he had put the canteen to his lips, the judge pounded Fly on the back. Fly sputtered and coughed up the vile liquor.

A wicked look came into the judge's eye. The tiswin was making him mean. "You better pull your weight tomorrow, Shorty! You're not fooling us with that heavy breathing and gasping."

Fly looked at him through moist eyes.

"You don't work, you don't eat." Bull Whacker's glass eye stared right through him.

"Eat? There's hardly nothing left. How can I work all day and night on two bits of dried jerky. You boys been eating *six!*"

"We're bigger than you, Fly." The judge surveyed his small frame.

"But you expect me to do just as much digging!"

Bull Whacker took the tiswin, drank again. It dribbled from his lips.

"My wrists are swollen." Fly dropped his head into his hands. "My ankle's twisted in pain. I broke my glasses. I can't see. . . ." He was blubbering almost incoherently. "My eyes hurt—my head throbs all the time. I'm dizzy. I've been even spitting blood—why didn't I listen to the major? Oh, Jesus! Oh, Christ! . . ." He broke down completely. Sinking to the ground, he gave into tears. The two watched him. The judge looked at the crumpled heap of Fly. The sound of his weeping sent a disquieting chill through them. A chill almost as cold as the black, damp of the Caves.

". . . and two boxes of ammo," Gatewood said softly, "quarter bag of corn, two slices dried pork fat, half can mush, quarter bag of cawfee, what's left of one skinned mule—half a leg. Two bottles tiswin and half of a quart of whiskey, one pouch of dried beans, three ounces of tobacco, and five half-smoked cheroots—that's our lot."

The major's beard was thick, unkept. His eyes were red and raw. The air in the Caves made them itch, until he wanted to pry them out. "How long you figure our store will last?"

"Enough for two days," the sergeant added soberly.

"We'll make it last four. Got to. Gatewood, dole it out. You carry it from now on, too."

"You're the brass, Major." Gatewood stuffed the supplies into a gunnysack. It was barely half filled.

The major frowned. "I got feelings the Apaches are close." The major's intuition was right.

With a stick the old warrior drew a circle. Then, he set out several bones—human bones—in its center. These were the bones of his enemy. He offered up a short prayer of strength, a prayer of courage, a prayer in preparation, for the kill. . . .

"Ducks must've just wandered off." The sergeant had been so tired that he had taken little notice of anyone. They had made an attempt to locate the farmer. But, their weakened condition had limited it to half-hearted calling. The sergeant had gone back, but only a few hundred yards, afraid of being left behind.

"Well," the major said philosophically, "if he fell in a hole, I hope it was the same one his wife did."

Barrett sat hunched by the fire. The light was bad. He squinted as he wrote. His words picked up a tempo of their own. He soon found that the hunger pain in his stomach was a mere annoyance. The more he penned, the less he noticed it. At first his words were schoolboy scrawlings, much like his first rough attempts to form letters, then making words. Slowly a touch of coherence came to his thoughts. He was back in school in Boston under the wing of his tutors. By rote he scratched out his lessons, conjugating in Latin the word *free*. He filled a page and hastily flipped it as if afraid to lose his momentum. His Latin fled him. A troubled look furrowed his brow, as he stared at the blank page. The weight of confinement pushed him to write his name one hundred times as if in punishment. Joshua Langdon Hamilton Barrett. Then, one name at a time, he meticulously scratched each out.

"Why are we being spared?" Barrett mumbled as he wrote and scratched. "Men's lives aren't over because they die," his head swirled. "Oh, no, they die when their life is over," he whispered hoarsely to himself. Suddenly, he stopped, aware of someone approaching.

"Listen, here," the major squatted down next to him, glancing at the chicken scratches in Barrett's notebook. Barrett smiled at him vacantly, covering the page with his hands. "Words is your game, Barrett. I got the fastest gun in Fort Huachuca, but the slowest pen." He stopped, trying to see if Barrett understood him. His eyes were glazed and strange. "Suppose you could write a letter in my name to the mothers of the soldiers that got killed outside? I mean when we get out of here?" Barrett nodded curiously, coughed into a filthy handkerchief, giving the major a pause. "You know what to say, the usual shit, about his bravery— died for country, and so on and so forth. I'd appreciate that." The two men stared awkwardly at each other."

"Sure, Major," Barrett bobbed his head. It bounced like a senile old man's. He turned back to his notebook and continued writing.

The major coughed, breaking off. "Now don't lag behind. Hear? Keep up!" It looked like he would have to remind him later about the letter. He stood up. He watched the reporter for a few moments but he could have been a thousand miles away.

The troopers worked faster now. A tunnel penetrated the rock slide. It was nearly eleven feet deep and about four feet wide and high. At first they had been digging in the middle of the rock slide. But cave-ins were too frequent. Now, they worked at the top of the pile, digging down, scraping for the roof of the overhang. Five men were cramped in the tight quarters of the tunnel. The lieutenant looked at the half-naked, sweating men. Their faces were dirt-caked and eerily lit by the day's shadowy light and three smoke torches.

Orley chopped with a pick. His movements were awkward, and he could only swing with half his strength. As he worked each rock loose, he rolled it behind him, where another raw, gritty pair of hands lifted and passed it.

They coughed and grunted in rhythm with the hacking of the pick.

Only one torch lit the progress of those inside. They, too, had made a dent in their tomb. Their tunnel was only five feet deep and wide. The judge worked in the front of the hole. He braced his back on the wall for support. His shirt was ripped and his back was scratched and scabby. He used the leg of one of Fly's tripods as a pick. There had been quite a fight to get it from the little so-and-so, but in the end Fly had had no choice.

Bull Whacker was on his hands and knees. His nose was almost wedged into the judge's pantleg. From it came dripping globs of glistening slime oozed with blood, which he wiped continuously with the back of his hand. As the judge loosened each rock, Bull took it from between his legs and passed it back to the half-dead Fly. It took nearly ten minutes to move one stone.

They were constantly slowed up as the wall still shifted, sending up little clouds of choking, powdered dust. The judge clawed and pried at one weighty rock. Smaller stones tumbled at his feet as he wrestled. The rock was passed painfully down the line to Fly. He encircled the small boulder with his arms. Taking a deep breath, he hoisted it. Almost immediately, it sunk him. He could feel his bones cracking against each other as he pivoted and dropped it. Then he collapsed. He convulsively fought to catch his breath. The judge looked back at him with venom, staring hate at the little man.

Fly had been warned. He struggled back to his feet and waited for the next torturous load to come his way. As they worked, they all listened to the sound from the other side. It seemed more resonant, closer. Or was it their own noise? It didn't matter, the beat of the chipping kept them going.

It was chilly even around the campfire. The sleeping figures moved closer together. The major watched the fire and shivered. There was little wood left. He would have to get used to the cold. Soon there would only be enough for the torches. They would be finished without light. The light shafts from the ceiling were intermittent. It was his watch. Fatigue wore on him like the eternal limestone drippings in the Caves. It encased him like stone. His eyelids grew heavier. He picked up his rifle, hoping that the feel of cold steel would revive him. The weapon felt clammy. It slipped out of his hands. He let it slide back down beside him. . . .

High above, another watched the camp. Taza was known to be able to remain motionless for unending periods of time. Only his eyes had moved, since the major's group had set up camp below him. It was time. He cupped his hands to his mouth. A soft warble, like a faraway bird's, slipped through his lips. The sound drifted down.

Suddenly, one of the mules pricked up its ears. It listened, then brayed softly. Without hesitation, the mule broke out of its halter and raced away. The major jumped away from the wall. He could hardly believe his eyes. The warble came again. The other animals pricked up their ears, broke free, and moved off. The major grabbed his horse, which had been tethered not too far from him. The horse was straining to get away to answer the distant call. "Easy boy," he stroked the horse's neck. "Steady now." Then the call came again, and his gray began to strain and whimper under his hands.

"Talbot! Gatewood!"

They both came running, pulling their boots on as they ran. The shouts woke up some of the others, who bolted up. By then, all the other mounts had disappeared into the dangerous void that surrounded them.

The major tried to quiet his horse, who was still yearning to run to the strange, enthralling invitation.

The sergeant started to move off after the animals, but the major stopped him. "No. It's too late. Too dangerous."

"Damn!"

"Apaches?" Gatewood asked. The major nodded. They all stared off into the dark.

Suddenly, the sound of drums rose through the silence. They seemed to mock the party, a beat of triumph in them. Baby Doe sat up. Her whole body shook.

The major moved forward into the engulfing pitch. "Come on out!" he screamed. Then he fired his rifle once. It retorted. Its echoes momentarily drowned out the drums. Then out of the dark a shadowy Indian figure emerged. They took aim, ready to fire. The figure took form, as it warily walked into the flickering light of the fire. It was Dull Knife.

"It was him!" Gabe shouted. "He spooked the horses and mules off!" He cocked the hammer of his hunting gun.

The major shoved Gabe's gun down. "Dull Knife always sleeps with the animals."

"Sure, he prefers them to us!"

"Then, why didn't he stop them from running off?" Venable accused. He and Gabe edged towards the Indian.

Gabe took a hatchet from his belt. "I say we take no chance—let's scalp him. I can get one hundred silver pieces for his scalp as well as any other!"

Dull Knife quickly drew his knife and froze. He waited, staring at their every move. He was as ready to kill as they were.

The major stepped between them. "Without him we're dead!" He turned to the Indian and spoke in rapid Apache. The major's words calmed the Indian somewhat. But his eyes remained fixed on Gabe as did Gabe's on him. There was a deep animosity between the two. The string of scalps on Gabe's belt was reason enough for the half-breed.

Turning, Old Gabe hissed to Venable, "But, don't ever turn your back on the sonofabitch for a minute!" Dull Knife knew he could never turn his back on the scalper either.

No one would sleep that night. Reluctantly, the party limped back to their makeshift bedrolls. Baby Doe wrapped her blanket tightly around her. She covered her head with the blanket like a child trying to block out a nightmare. Barrett did the same. Old Gabe hunched close over the fire. He pulled his rifle close to him and kept his eyes on Dull Knife. The Indian had not moved. His eyes were also riveted on Gabe. Venable would sleep sitting up. Gatewood and the sergeant patrolled along the edge of the camp. They and the major had no desire to sleep. It had begun. The Apaches had made their move openly. There would be no rest for any of them from then on.

Eli Fly's legs would hold him no more. He sat, a rifle in his lap, and strained to keep his bleary eyes open. His head kept falling onto his chest. Each time he succumbed, it became harder to raise it up. He yawned incessantly. The stagnant air made him drowsy.

A streak of light from somewhere high above beamed straight down—directly into the open, false eye of Bull Whacker. Sleeping on his back, face up, his mouth snored. One eye slept. But, his glass eye was agape, staring at nothing.

High above them, at the crack in the roof, White Horse moved slightly. He reached down and silently felt for his bow. Each movement was measured. His eyes never left their target. Slowly, he shifted his position. Crouching onto one knee, he slipped an arrow onto the bow. His shadowy figure blended with the stone. A lean, muscled arm pulled back the catgut. His eyes narrowed, took aim. Then, he carefully released his deadly missile.

It stirred the air ever so slightly. A low whistle went across the camp. Fly looked up curiously as it sped above him. A scream. Bull Whacker tried to stand. His hand groped madly around him. The arrow was stuck clean through his glass eye, shattering it. Fly rose in alarm. He looked around confused and dazed, having been wrenched from a dream. The judge opened his eyes, gaped at Bull Whacker, then cautiously moved toward him. Their eyes darted around the semi-lit walls of the cave. Fly stared mutely in horror.

Bull Whacker continued to scream. His voice broke through the camp with chilling eerieness. Crawling to his knees he bellowed convulsively, "Oh, God!" Starting to totter, clutching the arrow, he began to fall, the word "*Je-sus!*" slipping from his lips again and again. His face twisted grotesquely against the cold rock floor. In desperation he ripped the chiseled arrow out of his eye. The Indians at last had closed forever his

Evil Eye. Blood gushed from his wound, pouring out of him and over his clothes and the stone. He shuddered spasmodically, then quietly, breathing heavily, in pain, slumped, clutching his face, trying to keep his life's blood from escaping.

The judge and Fly stared at his blood-soaked shirt and his hands through which a steady flow of the oozing red came. No one moved. No one could tear their eyes from the arrow, which he clutched angrily in his hand. Snapping out of his daze, the judge moved to Bull Whacker's side. Ripping some of his own shirt, he tried to block the gaping hole. Fly watched, his eyes wide. "Help, man!" The little man came to them, his limbs moving with reluctance as if in a nightmare. It was not the sight of blood which gave him cause to balk. His files were full of photographs of maiming wounds far more horrific than Bull's. He had seen men literally blown apart, men that were only trunks, their legs and arms left somewhere back on the battlefield, dangling in war-battered trees, floating in slimy, mud slick creeks. But his camera had separated him from the reality. The image was only that, a light impression on a photographic plate. Now no camera stood between him and the proof of the death surrounding them all.

"Fly!" The judge's urgency broke the shaken photographer out of his gaze. With trembling hands, Fly stopped next to Bull Whacker and began wrapping a filthy strip of shirt around Bull's head. He could not bring himself to look at Bull Whacker's face, which was grimacing with each awkward, clumsy move of Fly's unskilled hands. The rough-hewn cowman chewed his lip to stave off the pain.

Suddenly, the sound of drums split through the deadly pall. Fly dropped the tattered ends of the bandage and began to whimper. They all were riveted to the mocking sound, straining to see beyond the dim circle of light.

The judge saw some movement. "Up there!" he pointed his rifle up to the crack in the ceiling. "There's the Apache that shot you, Bull!" He wedged his rifle on his shoulder and started to take aim.

Bull Whacker, despite his wound, grabbed his gun and peered up into the light with his one good eye. He mumbled as he squinted to catch sight of the Indian. They scanned the ceiling for several long minutes but saw nothing.

"Gone!" The judge lowered his gun. Beads of sweat dripped into his eyes and mouth. Their attention returned to the unwavering sound of the drums. It seemed to come from all around them. They began to feel the awful effects of claustrophobia. The dark constricted their very breath.

"Where do you suppose he went?" Fly stammered, barely heard.

"Back into the rocks like a snake."

Overcome by a cold sweat, shivering, more frightened than ever in his life, Fly sank to the ground.

"But when he's ready, he'll be back."

He would be back. He was as persistent as the Reaper, it was only a matter of time. The Apache's arrow was as sure as the sickle of death; it would teasingly slice them all down to nothing. Fly groped away into the dark trying to flee his sinking thoughts. . . .

Chapter
Ten

The undulations of the drums rolled through the grottos and chasms like eerie voices of the dead. The sounds wafted against the walls filling every chamber with their awesome note. The frenzy and primitive unending beats in the foreboding black resounded and echoed with the wrath of the ancient Apache Gods. . . .

They had picked up what seemed to be a worn groove that wound its way along the rock. The stone was almost soft to the touch as if caressed by countless rawhide soles over the millenia. Without the pack mules, they had to carry the firewood themselves. They had tried to load it up on the major's horse for hours. But the animal would not stand for it. He became impossible to handle. The wood was too important to risk losing on a spooky horse. Struggling along the path, they looked like moving cactus on a midnight desert. Gabe's scalps dangled on him like Spanish moss. The wood rode his back like a skeletal cowboy. Venable's equipment clanged with each step. He was nearly doubled over from the weight. Like a shepherd and his sheep, the major stubbornly led them on.

All around them, the blanket of pitch maintained its vigil. Slipping through the dark, bouncing lightly on the walls, the unchanging rhythm of the drums engulfed them. The major pulled out a twig from the smoking kindling. His cheroot flared up as he sucked on it. But his eyes never left the perpetual night of the Caves.

Talking would only bring their fears into the open. It was better to leave them unvoiced, unheard, and perhaps, unrealized. The flames flared up, as the kindling ignited the one log in the sparse fire. The walls of the cavern sucked in the light and opened up the vast panorama of the roomlike curtains.

Looking around, the major finally spoke, "This is an Apache burial ground." The sound of his voice had startled them out of their own quiet. They abruptly glanced around the walls which were bathed in the flickering of the fire.

"Well, they're not going to bury *me* here, goddammit!" Stepping back instinctively, Gabe waited for their reaction to his breach of the silence.

"Bite your tongue, Brother . . . " the major said, ominously. They all apprehensively looked at Gabe, then turned their attention to the dark again. Their ears focused out into the void, listening for any whispers of their silent enemy.

Once the initial shock had worn off, Bull Whacker's bandaged eye caused him only a steady pain. The glass eye had cracked—but it had protected his head from the piercing end of the arrow, which had in fact, blunted and broken off. The side of his head was numb and troubled him when he rested. Then, too edgy to sleep, the pain raged like a crawling sore, eating through his body. Bull Whacker would rather work than let the wound engulf him. But now, only two could work the tunnel, because the third had to stand guard. The Apaches were with them. The broken, bloodied arrow was the evidence of their presence. There was no other sign.

Fly was at the head of the tunnel. They had dug almost ten feet. Mechanically, without thinking, without feeling, he pulled rocks, on his cut hands and scabby knees. He tossed stone after stone with dead arms. He could not even tell if the dampness on his hands was blood or sweat. His glasses lay smashed among the debris. Without them he was as good as blind. His impaired vision did not catch the building rancor in the judge's face.

Grunting and sweating profusely, from fever not exertion, Bull Whacker worked. Then he sat up and rested. As soon as he did, his head began to act up. The pain mingled with the fever. Shaking his head, Bull tried to dislodge the waves of broken spasms that gyrated across his eye. It was like desert blindness. Next thing, he would be seeing things. He rapped his forehead with his gritty unwashed, bloodstained palm, trying to knock some sense back into himself. Only one thing would cure his affliction. Stumbling to his knees, he started crawling back into the tunnel. He shoved past Fly who was on his way back out. As soon as he started lifting and digging, the pain subsided and his vision cleared. Sitting on his ass was no good. Hard work was the thing that kept him going.

The judge stood guard at the opening of their miniscule tunnel, rifle cradled in arm. He swigged from the canteen. The tiswin did not faze him, his stomach had grown immune to the acrid taste. Each time Fly emerged, the judge turned away. When unnoticed, he gazed stupidly into the canteen, letting the dulling tiswin spill over him. Liquor was long past a crutch, it had become his backbone. It seemed he had never been without a drink. Even as a kid, he had been spoon-fed home brew to ward off the evils and afflictions of living. The slightest ache or complaint and out would come the bottle. By the time he was twelve, he would invent a little ill and his ever-loving mother would make him swill that blessed brew down his gullet. Some folks said that liquor was a man's ruination. Tasker thought of it as his salvation by oblivion.

He leaned down into the hole to be heard. "When I was a judge, I fined every criminal by opening a mail order catalog, with my eyes closed." He moved aside as Fly crawled out with a stone. "Once gave a man a fine of $10.49 for stealing two horses. When he complained, I said, 'You're lucky I didn't open the catalog to pianos!' "

"Bet you never drew a sober breath on the bench, you

old fool!" Bull Whacker lifted and dug. The tunnel was filled with the smell of weeks of sweat and old urine. His hair and beard were drenched with it.

"Neither did the jurors." The judge shifted uneasily. "Hell, I once fined a dead man thirty dollars."

"Bet you took it out of his pockets yourself." Bull Whacker had no taste to listen to the judge ramble.

"Give me a break, Judge." Fly collapsed near his feet. "I need a couple of hours off." He coughed and choked. His eyes were glazed and red. "If you make me go on, it's a death sentence!" Judge Tasker was unmoved by the little man's misery. He sullenly looked away.

"If I don't get some grub, I'll be joining you!" Bull Whacker grumbled as he crawled out of the tunnel. He stopped halfway, still on his hands and knees. "Listen." They heard a cracking, rolling noise.

"What's that?" Fly looked around frightened.

Bull Whacker grinned insanely. "My stomach." They all gazed off into the tunnel, listening to the steady hammering of those outside.

After several long minutes, the judge kicked Fly, and motioned with his head for him to work again. Fly struggled to his feet. His legs barely held him. He steadied himself against the rocks, feeling his way a few feet. Each breath was deliberate. His throat and mouth and lungs were coated with the powdered residue of smashed rocks. He had to measure each intake of air. He wheezed and looked back to the judge. "You're a gambling man." The judge nodded and shoved him with his rifle butt. Fly asked seriously, "What's the chances of me making it out alive?"

Tasker studied him for a moment. Then, he said solemnly, "None at all." Bull Whacker stared at him, knowing that the Judge was right.

Their sleep had been undisturbed by anything other than their own nightmares. The wonders of the burial ground had given their spirits a much needed lift. They

114

explored it like eager children in a field of death, momentarily forgetting their own. Barrett's face was drawn and gaunt, but his eyes were once again alert, alive. His heavy beard bristled and glistened with grime. He stood before a chiseled Phoenix which covered a ten-foot wall. He leaned close to it. His fingers ran along the grooves of the stone carving.

"There's a whole history of Indian civilization right here." The major, next to him, examined the drawings.

"What a story this is going to make." Barrett started walking along the length of the huge room. He stopped in front of a bas-relief of a huge deer with an arrow-shaped gullet. He took out a crumpled notebook and made rapid notes. His face was getting that mad look again. He mumbled to himself as he wrote. Barrett was lost in the frenzy of discovery.

Talbot had gone further into the cavern. "Bones, human bones!" Dull Knife spoke a rapid staccato of Apache to the major. The sergeant pointed to a neat pile of bones and Indian artifacts.

"The Apaches bury them with all their worldly possessions," the major explained. "So nobody can inherit. That way, they believe, there's no reason to wish anybody dead. There's an old chief's horse's bones." The major touched a skull with his foot. "The skull faces west, where the sun goes down." He had no doubt that the old chief, whoever he was, now a skeleton, was riding in some faraway Indian heaven on the spirit of the horse's bones before them. The old chief's skeleton smiled and one bony finger pointed at the major. Pilcher shook his head to eradicate the vision. The old chief turned and rode off into the dark.

Major Pilcher began examining the objects around him. "I bet this has got a story in it!" He picked up a skull. An old iron hatchet was imbedded in it.

Dull Knife spoke again to the major. Then he moved off some ways with his torch. "He says we should leave the dead alone. It's sacrilege, and dangerous." He looked off after the scout's flickering light.

The major dropped the skull. It splintered and crumbled. He looked slightly unnerved. Suddenly Dull Knife called back to them. He pointed with his torch to a trunk. Beside it were old wooden trunks, many old boxes, and piles of women's clothes and debris.

The major pried open the trunk with his rifle barrel, started pulling things out of it. "Stolen boodle, uniforms, old newspapers, Pony Express mail!" The contents of the trunks soon were strewn all around.

Baby Doe's mouth fell open. "Dresses." She eagerly started pulling them out of a box, lovingly rubbing the dusty, silken material on her face.

"I guess this is Geronimo's secret cache, all right."

Dull Knife's Indian blood told him the grave robbers would pay for disturbing the dead. He moved further off, feeling safer with some distance between himself and these ghouls. Perhaps the dead would see he had no part in it.

Gabe found a silver-framed hand mirror. Baby Doe took the mirror from his hand. She looked into it. Not believing what she saw, she cleaned the glass with her sleeve. She stared into it again, then looked away. With the hem of her skirt, she tried to wipe the layers of dirt off her face. Then, she looked at her hair and gasped, "My hair!" A sick look came over her face. "My eyes are sunken—hollow." She stared without blinking. "Are those my cheeks?" Her eyes were empty and dull. The fullness was gone from her cheeks. She looked old. "I've aged *ten* years!" She hurled the mirror against a wall. It shattered.

The major opened up another trunk. In it were piles of papers and letters. Sifting through them, he stopped occasionally to read old, yellowed newspapers and magazines.

"Will you listen to this ad in *Harper's Weekly?* Elbert's Saloon: One dollar for first bath—fifty cents second, and same water—twenty-five cents third bath, same water—ten cents last water."

"And, none of us have had a bath in weeks!"

116

Sergeant Talbot said scratching his leg.

"I'd give anything for a hot bath, even the dime one," Baby Doe said wistfully.

Barrett stopped apprehensively in front of one mammoth cave drawing. His eyes could not be torn from it. Standing above him was a fierce, painted warrior, three times larger than life. The drawing stood guard over the ancient dead. One arm was ominously raised. In it was a spear, which was pointed directly at the marauders.

It was scorching hot. Too hot to sleep. Inside the fifteen-foot tunnel it was at least a little cooler. The shift schedule had broken down. Exhaustion was chiseled in their faces. The rescue chute was wide enough for three men to work side by side. The string of sweating arms passed the stones down the line. The lieutenant stood at the opening, his back hunched like a gnarled bush. Each stone plummeted and crashed to the floor of Skeleton Canyon. They looked like skulls.

The judge's breath came in short, rasping gulps. "Don't know how much longer we can go on." His head was spinning, his sight kept going in and out of focus. The all-consuming dark of the Caves seemed to be making him blind. "No food," he whined, "little water. . . ."

Bull Whacker clumsily shifted in the tight quarters. He stared off into the cave to Fly. "If only that little bastard would stop faking it." He smashed a rock into another. The limestone crumbled in his hand.

"It's just a goddamn cheap trick!" the judge snapped. Their faces dripped with sweat.

Eli Fly looked to be two steps from death. He was already corpse gray. His eyes were hollow, maddened. Strangely enough, he had changed into a suit. His derby hat hung over his tilted and emaciated head to his ears. His clothes draped on him so he looked like a human scarecrow. It had taken him a good deal of time

117

to set up his tripod. One leg of it had been broken off. He had had to prop it up on stones. He steadied the magnesium stand with one hand as he screwed his camera into the tripod.

"What's he doing?" Bull Whacker could not believe the bizarre scene.

"Fly!" Judge Tasker yelled. "You crazy!" Both men stood in their tracks. They stared at him, shaking their heads.

Fly paid no attention to them. He was in another world, far away from the Caves, far from life—or death. His mind was in a limbo. His body in an instinctive need to do something worked mechanically at the only thing he really had ever mastered. He tied a string to the release button on the dented camera. His fingers fumbled awkwardly. His joints were stiff, his knuckles bruised to a pulp. Slowly checking his equipment, he carefully propped the flare stand against the tripod. The whole contraption shook. He steadied it. Then he quickly stepped in front of the camera. A sick, half-demented smile crossed his face. He pulled the string. The magnesium flare went off. The camera snapped. His self-portrait had been made. A contented look came into his eyes. He slowly shuffled past the camera. The string was still clutched in his hand. As he headed towards his bedroll, the camera, tripod, and flare crashed down. The stand shattered, broken by Fly's own hand. The noise did not penetrate the fog in which he drifted. As a man walking into a church, he solemnly took off his derby. He placed it carefully beside the heap of rags on which he slept. Then, he slipped into his bedroll and peacefully shut his eyes.

The judge and Bull Whacker came to him. They stared down at his remote, half-smiling face. "There . . ." Fly mumbled softly, "my last picture. Now, my camera's eye is closed forever." He looked at both men with a frightening calm and serenity. "Let me sleep, boys." He closed his eyes and welcomed the dark that slipped over him.

Chapter Eleven

Had it been days or weeks since the avalanche? No one cared. They looked now more for food than anything else. The little energy they had was used up in catching bats, lizards, and snakes. And there before them was food—plenty of food—the major's horse. But the major stood between them and his animal.

Gatewood sat close to the small fire, a stick held into the flames. Gored through it were six bats roasting. Several more were hung on a string. They ravenously watched as the small, almost meatless lumps sizzled and burned. Much of their day had been spent in snaring the bats. They had caught enough for two days in a makeshift net—two sticks and a petticoat. The bats were so small it had hardly seemed worth the effort.

"How come the scout and those Apaches are such blood enemies?" Barrett squinted at the major. The bright fire blinded him. His eyes were not adjusting to the light as they should.

"Because of us. He's a half-breed. Half American, half Apache." Then he slowly grinned. "His mother was Indian, his father, engineer." Barrett wrote down the major's words verbatim. But he knew it was much deeper than that. Dull Knife still felt very alien to his half brothers. But the Apaches had never forgiven him for cutting off the squaw's nose. He was only a half-breed, but she had been full Apache.

"Bat meat?" Gatewood extended the stick around the group. "Who's first?"

"Give it here." Baby Doe tore off a piece.

The major looked at a charred lump. He stuffed the bony meat into his mouth.

"Mr. Barrett?" The corporal waved the stake under Barrett's nose. He took it without looking up, ate the meat without tasting. Hunger and weakness had cast a haze over his mind. He was not even sure anymore when he was walking or sitting still.

Venable grabbed his share, almost pulling the stick out of Gatewood's hands. He bit into it like a jackal. Hardly taking time to chew, he gulped, almost choking, as he swallowed. They devoured the meat not even balking at the peculiar flavor. They had to eat what the Apaches ate. Their supplies were gone.

"How come Dull Knife isn't eating?" Gabe spit out a bat bone. His beard was streaked with grease and bits of meat.

"Because you haven't offered him none." Major Pilcher motioned to the cook with his head. Gatewood pulled a skewered bat off and held it out to Dull Knife. The Apache, with no hesitation, took it. He pulled off a wing and crammed it into his mouth. He chewed loudly. The others stared in fascination. Dull Knife grunted between mouthfuls.

"Put more on the fire, Gatewood!" They were all quick to agree, wiping their fat-covered faces, then licking their hands. Gatewood speared two more bats from their next day's supply into the flames.

"Major," Baby Doe looked at the scout curiously. "Ask him—why he don't sit with us—close to the fire?"

The major asked Dull Knife. The Apache answered, waving a bat wing in one hand as he gestured. "He says," the major translated, "the White Man builds a big fire, but stands far away. Indian makes a small fire, stays close. It's better." Dull Knife went on, with Major Pilcher translating again. "The Apaches also say when the White Man hears gunfire, he rushes to the spot. When Apaches hear gunfire, they run the other way, then crawl back to look."

Gabe tipped his hat to Dull Knife. Then he took out a Jew's harp. He twanged it. Baby Doe began to stomp her feet and clap her hands. Gatewood and the major clapped their hands and began to sing, both out of tune. "Raised in the backwoods, suckled by a polar bear. . . ."

Sergeant Talbot wearily patrolled along the edge of the camp. He had never been too partial to singing. Only fools and preachers' wives kept a tune in their heads. The only songs he knew were hymns, and those he chose to forget, along with the memory of a boyhood of forced Bible reading. It had soured his stomach on the Lord forever. All the praying in the world would never stop a man from dying. It had not kept the typhoid out of his house. It had not kept the undertaker away. All his mother's religion did not stop her from dying hideously, screaming all the way as the fever in her head grew like a sick flower, finally snuffing out her sense, then her life.

She had died calling to God to stop the pain. But, God hadn't heard.

Barrett gazed into the fire, like an insect drawn to light. Gabe's tune, nor the singing reached his ears.

Venable sang, "Nine rows of jaw teeth, a double coat of hair. Steel ribs, wire guts and a barbed wire tail."

"And I don't give a dang where I drag it!" Baby Doe blurted out. They were all trying to force themselves to forget—even for just a moment.

The last dregs of the whiskey was passed. They were drunk, as much from their despair as the liquor.

Suddenly, Venable burst into a dirty song, directing it more or less at the only woman present.

> One, two, three, four,
> I don't care if I go crazy,
> Long as I can pull my daisy,
> I can't care if I die, die, die—
> Long as I can see it fly!

Baby Doe screamed. Old Gabe threw a damp cooking rag into his face. Venable hacked and then went on.

She stood out there,
In the midnight air—
And the wind blew up her nightie.
The moonlight lit,
On the nipple of her tit—
Oh, Jesus Christ A'mighty!

Suddenly, Old Gabe stopped. He put down his harp. "Here we sing like fools, while out there they're plotting to stamp out our lives."

Baby Doe's smile quickly left her. She rocked back and forth. Venable glared at Gabe for having fractured the spell. The major sat among them, thoughtful, remote. Again the dismal reality of their situation poured somberly over them all. The pitch of the Caves clung to them, drawing fear like flies into their overwrought imaginations.

"He's been like this all day." Fly's mouth hung limply open. He stared up at both men with glassy, lost eyes. "Still breathing," the judge watched his chest rise and fall imperceptibly.

"You all right, Fly?" Bull Whacker whispered close into his ear.

Fly moved his lips, but neither man could hear his words above the sound of the digging. Bull Whacker leaned over Fly's mouth. "Can't speak . . ." Fly muttered so softly, that Bull Whacker covered his other ear in order to hear it. "Can't move—can't get up . . ." Fly coughed weakly. A trickle of blood ran down his cracked lips over his purple, swollen tongue. "Sorry, boys. . . ." He did not have the strength to brush a mosquito from the corner of his eye. Blinked feebly. The insect did not move.

Slowly the images of the judge and Bull Whacker disappeared. He thought they were still there. He had not heard them move away. His eyes were open. At least he thought they were. But he could not see. He wanted to get up but he could not move. It was as though a weight held him down. His own weight. He had become so weak that he could not lift his own hand. A sweet, familiar smell drifted to his nose. Perfume. He remembered it now. New York. The actress. He could see her. She was smiling. At him? No, at his camera. They always smiled at his camera, never at him. She waved, blew him a kiss. He watched himself get up and walk to her. He left his cameras behind. . . .

The major saw their depression—he thought he would lift them up. "Well, I almost got killed a dozen times. To my dying day, I'll never forget one." They all looked up at him, eager for him to go on. "One day, I was riding alone, about ten miles from the fort. Suddenly, I was surprised by a savage Indian brave in war paint. Putting spurs to my horse I tried to escape. The Indian, mounted on a fleet pony, quickly followed me in pursuit. My only weapon was a six-shooter. The Indian pursued me relentlessly and refused to be shook off. We were nearing the edge of a deep and wide gorge. No horse could leap over that awful chasm, and a fall to the bottom meant certain death. I turned my horse suddenly, and the Indian was on me. We both fired once, an' both horses were killed. We now engaged in a hand-to-hand conflict with knives. He was a powerful Indian—tallest I ever saw. It was a long and fierce struggle. One moment, I had the best of it, and the next he did." Here, the major paused, as if to get his breath.

"How did it end?" asked Baby Doe.

"Why, the Indian killed me!" the major replied with slow deliberation.

They all laughed—breaking the spell, realizing he had been joshing them.

Finally Venable, not to be topped, began, directing himself mostly to Baby Doe. "Well, I seen some things in my travels. A petrified forest, as sure as my rifle's got hindsights and she shoots center. I was out on the Black Hills—the year it rained fire—and everybody knows when that was. The snow was about five-foot deep, and the buffalo lay dead on the ground like bees after a bee-ing; not where we was though. There was no buffalo and no meat, and me and my band had been living on berries for six weeks; and poor doings that feeding is, as you can guess. One day we crossed a canyon and over a divide where there was green grass and green trees and birds singing, and this in February!

"Our animals were like to die when they see the green grass, and we all sung out, 'Hurray for summer doing's.' 'Here goes for meat,' says I, and I just up old Ginger at one of them singing birds and down come the creature elegant, its darned head spinning away from the body, but the bird never stops singing. When I took up the meat, I find it stone. Wagh! 'Here's damp powder and no fire to dry it,' I says, quite scared. 'Fire be dogged!' says my partner. He takes his ax and lets drive at a cottonwood. *Schr-u-k* goes the ax against the tree and out comes a bit of the blade as big as my hand. We look at the animals, and there they stood shaking over the grass, which damned if it wasn't stone, too. I scraped the trees with my butcher knife and snaps the grass like pipe stems and I break the leaves like shells. 'What's all this?' I asked my partner. 'Petrified,' says he, looking smart, 'we have found a whole petrified forest.' "

"Yes that's the way it is when they go by starving." The judge gazed down at Fly's flaccid face. The little man's eyes were closed, but his chest still moved with sporadic breathing. "That'll be us, in a few days. . . ."

"Maybe, they'll get here?" Bull Whacker glanced with small hope at the Caves' entrance.

"Can't help them much." The judge forlornly shook his head. "Too tired." Speaking was taking too much out of him. He mumbled words, not sentences. "Digging, keeping awake, watching, guarding," his voice lowered to a bare whisper. "No sleep, too weak. . . ."

"Unless?" Bull Whacker stared at the judge. He took his pistol out of his gunbelt, put it in the judge's hand, aimed the gun at Fly's head.

"I can't, Bull . . ." the judge dropped his arm. The pistol trembled against his leg. "Can you?"

Bull Whacker took the gun. "I killed before. It's better like this." He did not look at the judge, who stood next to him, terror in his eyes. "Put him out of his misery."

"Then? Bury him?"

Bull Whacker lifted the gun in answer. He steadied his aim with both hands. The judge walked away. His legs were too weak to run. His heart jumped so much that it almost knocked him over as the shot rang out.

The major's party had rested fitfully. It had been only a short while that morning until they stopped again. Their eyes slowly became accustomed to the blinding sunlight. It poured down over them from a narrow, twisting passageway. At the end of it, they could see blue sky.

"Sky! Blue sky!" Gabe cried. He hugged Venable. They danced around in a mad circle. Baby Doe sank into Barrett's arms and squeezed him as tightly as life. Tears rolled down her cheeks. She turned to the major and hugged him. They held each other for a moment. She joyously kissed him. Their ordeal was over. They were free.

Gatewood threw his hat on the ground and stomped on it, then pointed up. "The way—*out!*"

A "Yah-*hoo!*" came from Venable's lips.

"Yowie!" Talbot let loose a rib-rattling Texas rebel yell. No weakness, no hunger was felt by any of them.

Slowly, they subsided, stopped, and watched as the major scrambled up the rift in the granite. They held their breaths. Suddenly, about half way up, the major stopped.

"What's wrong, Major?" Gatewood's voice skidded over the surface of his fears.

"Just one damn thing," the major yelled as he slowly wormed his way back down. "How are we going to get up there?" Their triumph was quickly dashed, the bitter sweetness of victory short-lived.

"What you mean?" Gabe shouted, not willing to face defeat after all this outburst.

"Can't you see, man?" The major dropped down the last few feet. He faced them all with disappointment, "It's too goddamn small, too *tight*. . . ." They all stared up dumbly. It had become very quiet. Sagging dejectedly to the floor, they stared up at the teasing blue sky. No one said a word for quite a while, feeling like the leader in a race who fell a few feet from the finish line. The race was forever lost.

"I can do it, Emmett!" Baby Doe stood up, breaking the silence. The men looked at her stupidly, curiously, half in wonder.

"That's out of the question."

Baby Doe laughed. "I'm the *only* one small enough— you boys are just too big!"

"I couldn't let you, Baby Doe." He looked at her seriously.

"Why not? You afraid of letting a woman save your neck?"

"It's just *too* risky!"

"Saying that you got out," Talbot looked at her dubiously, "what are you planning to do then?"

"Get help."

"How do we know you'd come back at all?" Venable asked. In all of his experience, women always ran when the fire got hot. They had memories as short as a gnat's leg. If she got out, that would be the last they ever saw of her; he would bet his life on that.

"On my life—I wouldn't desert you boys. You been too good to me!"

"So you figure you can walk forty, fifty miles, with no food, no water, and plenty of hostile Indians?" the major asked cynically, "then turn around, come back here to these hills and find that hole?"

"You have a better idea? At least I'll bring horses. Food."

126

"No, Baby Doe." The major took her arm. "It's better if we all stay together." A woman could never face up to the desert on foot. Her skirts alone would kick up hoards of sand crawlers, Gila monsters, sidewinders and scorpions. She would be bit, stung, and poisoned inside of a mile. If the desert didn't get her, the Apaches surely would. The white man's greatest fear was to lose a woman to the Apaches. Those that had come back from the most unspeakable of ordeals were never again right. Their minds were snapped, their souls wretched out of their bodies. The scars which marked their faces for life were badges of defilement. They were shunned by their own kind, because their ways had become so strange. He could not take the risk of sending her to an earthbound damnation. A man could deal with it, a woman could not.

"But, don't you see?" she pleaded. "This is the *only* chance we got. Nobody's ever going to find us if we keep wandering around in here. At least, if *one* of us gets out. . . ."

The major cut her off, still shaking his head. "No. there's another way out. I know it. The Apaches didn't use this way either. We'll find the way out—the *real* one!"

"Emmett," she said softly. "Let me do this, please. I want to. . . .'

He stared at her a long moment. Then, decided. "No."

"Up there is life," she pointed. "Down here, we can all die. I'm going. That's all there is to it. You can help me. If you don't—then I'll do it on my own!" This time she would not be swayed. All her life she had been treated like a china doll by her men and their smothering protection. Time and again she had been told what—as a woman—she could not do. Always the reasons were strength or that intangible cliche that it was not a woman's place. More often than not, she had let herself be pulled along in the fruitless guise of femininity, cushioning the loss of self-respect with fril-

127

ly gowns and fancy homes. She would prove she was as scrappy a fighter as any of the men stuck with her in the Caves. Let them swallow their pride for a change. Let a woman be the hand that pulls them out of their misery.

She seemed so determined. All at once he gave in against his better judgment. "All right." He handed her a rope. She tied it around her waist. He retied it, making the knot secure. He lifted her up on top of a thin rock ledge. "Talbot, stay sharp. Keep the others between you and the passageway." The sergeant nodded and assumed the guard. Then she and the major began the climb together.

The first twenty feet were easy. They crawled on their hands and knees all the time, moving toward blessed daylight. Then, the going became more difficult. The rocks pressed closer together. They soon were dragging themselves on their bellies. There were still sixty more feet to the top.

"This is as far as I can go, Baby Doe." The major tugged on the rope. She stopped, craned over her shoulder. "I can't talk you out of this?"

"Nope," she smiled confidently. "Wish me luck, Emmett!"

She turned to continue her climb. The major called softly, "Make it, Baby Doe!"

Winking at him, she blew him a kiss. "I'll be back—you still have to show me Tucson!"

The rocks were rough. Jagged edges stuck out like the iron teeth of a bear trap. There were few toeholds. As she squirmed and scraped up, it became harder and harder. Her struggle was intense. The others below strained with her. Their faces winced each time she slipped. She continued pulling herself further up, inch by inch.

Suddenly, she stopped. "Can't go no higher, Major!" She gasped for breath.

"It's just ahead, Baby Doe—fifteen more feet! You can do it!"

She inhaled deeply. Her hand groped up toward the light. Her foot searched for a toehold. Her leg brushed up against a jutting rock about level with her knee. She lifted her foot and braced on it. Her shoulders were packed together, sore and scraped.

"Keep going! You're almost there!" the major shouted, struggling with her every move.

She pushed with all her might, propelling herself roughly up a few more feet. Her back, her shoulders, her sides were crushed against the rock. Again, she found a toehold. Again she smashed her body up—up to the light. Once more, her hip bones grated against stone. She squirmed to ease the pain but only caused more.

"Can't!" she gasped.

"Ten more feet!"

"It's no use!" She rested her forehead against the cool shaft. She fought to slow her breathing. Deep breaths only further slammed her ribs into the rocks.

The major stared up at her, swallowing his chagrin. After a pause, he yelled, "Come back then!" She started to nod in reply. Her head cracked against the wall. She winced. After a moment, her energy collected, she started back. Her eyes glared bitterly at the inviting sky. She shoved with her hands. Nothing. She pushed again. And again. Her face glistened with perspiration, her eyes with a sudden—terrible fear. Starting to scream, she caught herself. Fighting to calm down, she forced herself to relax. Then, she tried again. With all her concentration focused on her hands, she pressed against the stone. It was no good. "I'm stuck!" She screamed, "I can't move! I'm stuck!" Her panic was rising.

"Oh, Je-sus!" The major gaped up at her. "Steady, Baby Doe!" He tried to be heard above her hysteria. "Don't move!"

Barrett whispered tensely, "She almost made it."

"An Apache could," Gabe muttered.

"No, I don't think so," Sergeant Talbot whispered

back. He had heard stories of Apaches sprouting wings and flying with the eagles, of turning inside out and changing into coyotes. Some folks even swore that Apaches could walk through walls and disappear off the face of the earth, only to turn up howling and spouting fire at a neighbor's ranch. Apaches were said to do a lot of strange things, but no man, red or white, could crawl through that snake hole.

"You men help me!" the major said restraining his own voice. "We're going to pull you down, Baby Doe!" She was whimpering. "Baby Doe, listen to me! Y' hear me?"

"Please, get me down!" The pity in her voice was undeniable. They were moved and shaken. But how does one control panic? It was the body's natural instinct. It flooded over her. Her heart raced, pounded in her ears, her throat.

"We will!" The major turned to the others. "Gabe, Talbot—help me with the rope." He yelled up to her, "Just relax, now. Be real still. We're going to pull you loose." The major scrambled up into the cleft, as far as he could go. He was cramped and wedged, and needed the other men's strength. "All right, boys—pull—nice and easy." They tugged the rope gently. Then harder. "Is it budging?"

The pressure on the rope worsened the pain. She could feel her bones crunching and chipping against the walls of her snare. Blood soon began to flow with her sweat. "You're killing me!" They immediately dropped the rope.

Her scream of agony had all the ring of truth in it.

"What the hell do we do *now*, Major?" the sergeant called up. The men beside him scarcely breathed. Their sweating faces were vacant. They had not the slightest hint of what to do.

"Try again! Please, Baby Doe!"

"No, I can't take it!"

"You've got to!" He tried to climb up to her. It was useless. He could not go a foot further. There were fifty feet between them. "We're going to do it again—push when I pull! Push for all your worth!" He started to pull again. They desperately jerked the rope and hauled.

"You're pulling me apart!" she sobbed. "Please, don't," she cried in dark despair.

The major helplessly slid back down to the rest. They were silent, glum, and very afraid. Major Pilcher walked off by himself, his mind reeling. Her cries made it impossible for him to think straight. There had to be a way.

She was in so much pain, she had become impassive, seemingly drugged and in a stupor. Too weak to struggle anymore, she went limp. "Don't leave me, please." Her deadened, torpid words drifted down to the others. "Men always leave me." They looked up guiltily. "I don't want to die," she mumbled incoherently. "I want to live—still young—got my whole life." The brackish dark was growing with each breath. "Don't leave me. Wait. . . ."

"We're waiting, Baby Doe!" the major called up. There was little else he could do.

"We're not leaving!" Barrett shouted loudly to hide his own despair.

"Hang on!" Talbot called up, but in his heart the sinking feeling grew.

"Baby Doe, you in pain?" the major asked futilely. It took her a long while to answer. They stared up the shaft. Her body blocked all but a tiny sliver of sun.

Finally, she murmured, "Pain. Yes. . . ." Then again, "Don't leave me! God, don't let them. Men always—leave me—please don't!" Then her head slumped down against the stone. . . .

She had fainted, the body's natural way of shutting off reality, beyond the limit of her mind to conceive.

And that reality was Death. . . .

But she did not just die—no, she slept. Slowly inching her way across the gulf, between this world—and the unknown.

And as she slept, she dreamt like a child dreams. She

was a young girl. She was walking barefoot back from school, a six-mile walk along winding, country roads and fields. Somewhere, there was green lush grass and love in the afternoon among the trees and against them.

The boys had different faces, different names.

They drifted before her.

She had always needed so much love. Why? Why so much?

As she slept—the young girl walked her way over the wooden bridge at the end of the gulf. Her mother quietly took the child's hand—and led her home. . . .

Chapter Twelve

Thirty feet. In God knows how many weeks. The excavation now had a much greater risk of cave-ins. In the canyon, game was scarce. The only thing that kept them going was the sound of life from inside, the sporadic chipping of the entombed.

Judge Tasker's snores wafted out of the ten-foot tunnel. The sound made Bull Whacker uneasy as he stood guard. But all his eyes could see was the body of Fly. A swarm of insects worked over the corpse. Bull Whacker had been staring at him for hours. Slowly, as if he were walking in a graveyard, he crept over to the crumpled human heap. He dropped to his knees. His body shook. After many long moments, he touched Fly. His hand sprang away from the cold flesh, as if he had been burned. He felt he was being watched.

Fearfully, he looked around, listened. The judge's snores were even and calm now. He touched Fly's arm again. The feel of flesh, of meat, made his mouth water. Without hesitation, he unsheathed his knife and plunged the blade into Fly's chest. He ripped the knife along the cavity. He had gutted many deer and buffalo this way. It seemed no different. His hands moved by themselves. He kept his eyes only on the succulent flesh. He tried not to see Fly's prim waistcoat. He kept his back to Fly's head. Suddenly, tears began to run down his face, but he did not stop. No one could condemn him. The knife scraped against bone. With shaking hands he grasped the rib cage and pried it apart.

"We haven't heard a sound out of the lady all day

133

long." The major's eyes were moist. "And all last night. . . ." His neck was cemented with a crick from staring up into Baby Doe's tomb. He had not slept, nor touched the meager rations that had been offered him. His hands were raw from fighting with the rope. He had pitted everything he had to rescue her. Now all that lay at his feet was the coil of rope. It had frayed against the stone and plummeted down. Their only link with her still body had been irretrievably broken.

"We been sitting here for almost two days. Just looking up."

"She's passed out, for sure." Gabe was casually going through her belongings.

Barrett beat his fist to the ground. Barrett pointed an accusing finger at the major. Then he weakly slumped back. "It's too awful!"

The major shuddered, with deep, halting sorrow. "Everyone's dying is awful. Hers wasn't too bad." His throat was thick. "Just like sleeping, drifting away." For the first time he felt real discouragement. He had become powerless to the Caves. Barely a hundred feet above was a woman who had touched a part of him. He was alive. She was dead. He felt emasculated and lame. All that remained for him was to face her eternal scorn.

"Hell, she went out fighting like a cat." Gabe was tired of hanging around for a dead woman. He got up, started getting his pack together.

"It used to happen in London to the chimney sweeps," Barrett faltered. "I read it in a book. Little kids, they'd get stuck and be left." He had not been able to hold down the bat meat. Hunger was making him ramble.

"This isn't no book, Mr. Barrett. It's life."

"No, it's not anymore, Major," the sergeant looked at him. "But it was. . . ."

The major walked a few hundred feet away from them sinking to the ground on his knees. Not since he had learned of his brother's death had he felt so

134

helpless. Then, as now, there had been no place to turn for solace. His grief would be borne alone, his shredded emotions shared with no one. He chose solitude. An anguished moan erupted from the depths of his being, torn from his bowels by the fist of despair. He wrapped his arms around himself. His lips turned white where he bit them. Then, he brought forth for his personal agony a release of choking sobs.

He would not be able to sleep for days and when he would, out of exhaustion, he would dream of her. Yes, for all the nights of his life, he would never stop dreaming of her. And in countless years to come, she would be his nightmare—his obsession—part of his deep-rooted, never-ending guilt.

But, he was not given time to mourn. The Caves would not allow him his grief. Suddenly, through his tears, he saw movement. Something was crawling and moving from rock to rock. He could barely make out the figures. Then, he could dimly see two rifle-carrying Apaches. Lifting his gun, he took aim and fired. His shots echoed. Then, silence. He peered into the dark. Then, quickly rising, he ran, plunged back to the living.

Off in the shadows before them were two figures. They sensed them more than saw them. Two Apaches were teasing them. The figures scrambled from rock to rock. Their rifles reflected the light in the cave, which they had become wed to like the bats.

The party was crouched behind a low wall of rocks, their muzzles pointed out at the half-shadowy figures. They waited. The game the Apaches were playing was effective. The men were shattered.

"Now you see 'em, now you don't." Sergeant Talbot's face was twitching again. For once he was thankful for the dark.

"At least, we know they're there," the major said, still shaken by Baby Doe's death. It took a lot out of a man, more so from a man who held his emotions so rigid. He was strangely relieved that the Apaches had loomed into view. For once, their timing suited the need of his raw emotions. "I'd just as soon fight it out with them now than wander around in here till it's maggot-sucking time. Geronimo's just too damn sure we'll never find the way out." He knew the old warrior well. He had sensed all along that this was his game.

Gabe cocked his rifle nervously. In his other hand was his scalping knife. He was taking no chances.

Sergeant Talbot whispered hoarsely, "They're close."

Venable was crouched so low he was almost prone on the ground.

"Why don't they shoot?"

"Why don't you, Gabe?"

"Because I can't see a thing!"

"Well, neither can they."

"Thought they could see in the dark like cats?"

"Maybe these aren't Indians," Barrett said deliriously. He sat with his back to the wall. "Maybe there's nothing out there except our minds playing tricks." Indeed, his imagination had carried him beyond the limits of the wall. He was hardly aware of what was going on around him. Sayings curled around the dark recesses of his mind, but none were complete. Disjointed quotes, unfinished lines bobbed inside his head like corks riding an incoming tide. Nothing quite made it to shore, nothing came to an end. "To be wise, and to love, exceeds man's. . . ." "It is a characteristic of wisdom not to. . . ." Not to . . . love? No, that was not how the line read. "The fault, Horatio, is not in the stars, but. . . ." In what? What fault? The major's fault. Yes, that was it. Barrett smiled, pleased that he had solved the riddle, had found the tag to end the line. Then he was brought back to reality with a thud.

"There!" Gabe pointed his rifle. "Saw one—thirty foot off!"

"They're closing in," the major turned to Talbot. "You and Dull Knife get my horse down!"

He and Dull Knife moved away from the cover of the

wall. They pulled the animal down. It remained on its side, as it had been trained to do. Then they crawled back to the others. Just as they did, a shot rang out. Then another. Then, a volley of shots splattered around them. The major fired into the dark. They fired a huge barrage at the unseen stalkers. The sounds echoed wildly like fireworks.

The sergeant yelled over the noise, "Better to die than live like rats!"

"Speak for yourself," Venable said cynically. I'd rather *live* like a rat!"

Suddenly, they realized that they were the only ones shooting. The major waved his hand. There was nothing out there.

"Anybody hit?"

The sergeant looked down the line. "Not here," he turned, then added slowly, "except, Major—your horse."

The major ran back, crouched next to the animal. Its head was in a pool of blood. He stroked the horse's neck. It struggled, trying to lift its head.

"Still alive. But not for long."

"Leave me, Talbot." Slowly, the major took out his pistol. He gazed at his animal for a long moment. Its haunches had become bony. Its ribs jutted out, piercing the skin. Its coat was no longer sleek but dull and matted. Patches of hair had fallen out. His hands shook as he lifted the pistol to the horse's head. Kentucky seemed far away, so far that he would never see the blue grass again. One bullet would bring an end to the only dream he had ever allowed himself. To rebuild his father's horse ranch had been a fool's notion, a passing fancy that had lingered too long. The major closed his eyes and squeezed the trigger killing the dream.

"You know something," Gatewood whispered to Barrett. "I believe the Apaches weren't tryin' to hit us—but just the horse."

"What's the point of that?"

"Point be to burn the major up, make him lose his

calm." Gatewood figured that Geronimo knew how much love the major had for that horse. He remembered when he ran off half the fort's remuda, including the major's horse. Not one man in the Fourth, not even the cook, had had a minute's rest until the gray had been back in the stable. The Apaches were not sentimental about horses, only used them and thought of them as food. So when the remuda had stampeded, they had not bothered to chase after them. Some Mexican wetback had found the major's horse wandering in the hills. He probably was still cursing the day that animal came into his life. He had been plowing a field, a crude harrow hitched behind the gray, when the major had ridden up. It had taken three troopers to pull the major off the screaming peon. Gatewood had been one. The unknowing horse thief had fled back to Mexico and never returned, as far as Gatewood knew.

Suddenly, there was movement in the dark again.

"They're going!" They all caught a brief glimpse of two Apaches moving off.

The major jumped on the wall and crouched. The sergeant and Dull Knife followed him. Corporal Gatewood started to go, but stopped. He leaned against the wall for support. No one else moved. The major dropped back off the wall. "Well, are the rest of you boys coming or not?"

From the look on their faces, the question was redundant. Venable straightened up. "I haven't lived this long by luck!"

"Without me, you'd all be dead by now."

Barrett suddenly scrambled to his knees, his eyes shining. "And what about Baby Doe? And the Ducks? You let them die!"

The sergeant defended him. "Baby Doe wanted to come so bad, she offered to pay her way."

"To kill her?"

"The Ducks' farm was burned to the ground. We had to take them!" He went on. Then the major turned to the corporal. "Gatewood?"

"You ordering me, Major?" Gatewood asked slowly. "If you are," his voice was shaky, "you're ordering me to die. I'm no fighter, I'm a cook." The corporal was visibly shaken. He had never held a gun until they had slapped the blue uniform on his back. After a while, when it had become clear that shooting would never be his forte, they had promoted him to cook, first class. The first class had always tickled him. Before the army had taken him in, he had never even been considered third class, just another ass to kick. The major had been good to him, had treated him like any other trooper, but now he was asking him to act like one, too. Gatewood felt a fierce loyalty to the man, but suddenly he was very unsure. "I can't hardly shoot, but if you want me, I'll try."

"Better stay then." The major looked down at Barrett who had huddled back against the wall. "What's your excuse, Barrett?"

Barrett squinted up at him. He was having trouble focusing. "Fightin's not my job."

"But living is?"

"Major, you wouldn't even begin to understand." Barrett tried to stand up, but was having difficulty. He slumped back down. "Go read my newspapers, my columns. I don't believe in killing!"

"But you believe in dying?"

"I believe in my *own* death only!" Barrett seemed far away, like a man afflicted with senility. "It's between me and my God."

"What a lot of balls," Gabe hissed. "He's just plain yellow—like me!"

The sight of them wallowing in cowardice revolted the major's sensibilities. They were nothing more than leeches on his back. The Caves would soon take care of them. If they had given up, so be it. He had no intention to. Looking over the emaciated and pitiful group, he spit. Then, turning his back on them, he started to climb over the wall.

The major jumped down the other side. Sergeant

Talbot slipped over the wall after him, rifle in hand. Dull Knife and then suddenly Gatewood followed, too.

Gatewood clutched his pistol and turned momentarily back to the others. "So long, boys—if I never sees you again!" He soon was lost to the shadows.

Bull Whacker and the Judge had taken the step that removed them from all salvation. Their eyes, their faces were warped. Both wondered what they had done to bring them to this. Their stomachs were full. Hunger had been appeased. A mortal fear for their souls gnawed at them far worse than starvation. They gazed at the fire. Hanging above it on a tripod was a leg and a human arm. The hand bent accusingly at them. At times, it even seemed to move, to point. Bull Whacker reached out and slowly turned the spit. With gaping mouth he stared at a wooden rack. Hanging on it to dry out was the rest of the evidence of their damnation. Dangling on strings were the remains of Eli Fly. Another leg, a foot, a thigh. But his heart, like his life, was gone. Eaten. Silently, in the dark, Bull Whacker could swear he still heard it beating. He listened wondering how in the name of sweet Jesus he could ever shut the damn thing off?

Chapter Thirteen

The major, Sergeant Talbot, and Gatewood groped through the dark. They had not taken a torch—to do so would have been plain stupid and sure death. Even so, the Apaches held the advantage; they knew where they were, the troopers were blindly lost. Spreading out a bit, they moved a few feet, stopped, listened. There was a patter of feet. First it seemed to come from one place, then another. Then, the echoes bounced around them, totally confusing the direction of the sound.

Gatewood strained to see, the whites of his eyes apprehensive in the pitch. A body moved. Then another. Something was behind him. He whirled around to face the sound, pistol cocked, ready to fire. He saw a flash of legs. Suddenly, off to his right there was a flash.

Talbot and the major flattened at the first explosion. Sweat rushed down the sergeant's face as he waited for the attack. The clenched muscles in his legs quivered. They had lost sight of one another. Being totally alone, not knowing if it were friend or foe in the shadows, played a toll on their imaginations. The major's mind wandered back to Baby Doe. Crouching in the darkness he could almost feel the kiss she had blown to him. He brushed his cheek, feeling an icy chill on his skin.

The quiet was broken by a low moan. The major jolted at the sound, startled out of his ghostly reminiscing. Someone had been hit. The sergeant was the first to move. He inched his way toward the source of the faint cry to see if their luck had changed, if they had downed Geronimo.

Suddenly, Talbot sagged. He felt as though he had

141

been smashed by a hammer. At his feet, he saw who had taken the bullet. Gatewood. He was slumped on the ground, clutching his stomach. Blood had soaked through his army-blue shirt, which clung to his chest in oozing purple hues. His black, pink-palmed hands were coated sticky and dripping. "Damn!" He grimaced as the sergeant knelt beside him helplessly. A spasm rocked his body. He clutched himself, trying to hold back the life that poured out of him.

The major came through the wall of dark. He lifted Gatewood slightly, bracing him against his shoulder. He glanced at his belly, ripped open as if by an enormous razor-edged scoop.

"I'm here, Gatewood." He wiped some dirt from the cook's brow, leaving a bloody smear in its stead. He could not bring himself to look in Gatewood's eyes, afraid of condemnation. But there was not time to pause for regret or think of guilt—the man was bleeding to death. He glanced around to find something to plug up the wound, but stopped as the soldier gripped his arm.

"Listen—promise you'll bury me. . . ." The major started to interrupt, to tell him there would be no need for a burying, but Gatewood's grip grew tighter. "Bury me good—under a pile of rocks." A fear, almost greater than of death itself, pushed him to get the major's word. It would be worse than a fiery purgatory to have his body tampered with once he was gone and could not look after it. Apaches pretty much let dead men rest, but a hungry man was liable to do anything to keep from starving.

Then his whole body wracked with one last convulsion, stiffened, and slumped. The major studied Gatewood's flaccid, unmoving features, as if waiting, hoping, to see the eyes open once more. Then he looked up, cursing God under his breath. He gently put Gatewood down and closed his lifeless eyes. Neither man spoke. The sergeant only gazed out into the dark void. The emptiness was building within them.

"First Baby Doe, then my horse, and now my old Gatewood!" A pained rumble broke the spell. "It's just too goddamn much!" Then with madness in his eyes, he ran off into the dark maze of the Caves.

Major Pilcher had been swallowed. The sergeant called desolately after him. "Major!" But only his voice came echoing back. . . .

All but one small bunch of wood had been used up. It had grown cold. For all they knew, the major and the others would never return. And then there was the horse. The smell of fresh meat had erased the major's warning from their famine-washed minds. They had ripped open the carcass without even uncinching the girth. Gabe had drunk the gushing blood. It had made him drunk. One stirrup had fallen between the fleshless ribs. It flapped in the gutted cavity, like the clapper of a bell. A leg, which jutted skyward, looked as though it had been gnawed—so great had been their haste.

They looked like scavenger rats as they huddled closely around the fire; their faces were streaked with grease, fat, and blood. Dripping, half-cooked hunks of meat—horsemeat—were in their dirty hands. Their clothes hung on them like rags. Their unwashed beards were crawling with lice. They watched each other suspiciously so that no one took more than his share.

Over the fire, a huge shank of horse roasted. They had not even bothered to skin it. Its gray hair had singed and now dotted the skin with black stubble. It turned on the spit. Hot, sizzling fat splattered into the fire and onto the ground. The bottom half was burnt, the top hardly cooked at all. Everyone was too busy eating to cook. So busy, in fact, that no one looked up to the sound of running.

Talbot dashed across the lighted area from the dark. Emotionally and physically wasted, he fell back against the wall of rocks and rubble. His nostrils flared. His stomach began to churn as the smells which filled

143

the camp drifted over to him. He was ravenous. The half-cut-up horse carcass was there for the taking. "Couldn't even wait!"

"Wait for what?" In Venable's hand was a juicy chunk of meat and bone.

"The cook?" Gabe sputtered through a mouthful. A piece of fleshy horsehair dangled from the corner of his mouth. Their eyes were glazed from the feast.

"Gatewood's dead."

Venable slowly lowered the piece of meat from his mouth. He self-consciously wiped his face on his sleeve.

Barrett dropped his half-chewed portion. "Damn!" It thudded and rolled a few feet. "*Damn!*" He covered his head with his hands.

"Suddenly I lost my appetite." Gabe looked at the meat. He thought for a second, then offered it to the sergeant. Talbot shook his head. Gabe insisted and put it in his hand. "We was really and truly dying of hunger. Sorry about your friend."

Venable mumbled, shook his head. "Just proves only the good dies."

Talbot gazed at the food. Yet, he could not eat. He looked through the fire seeing Gatewood. Many faces passed before his eyes. All his dead comrades. His generation had been born into war, raised in war, and sprouted into manhood carrying a gun. And yet he had never grown used to any man's death. One would have thought a soldier would have hardened to killing. But each time a man fell, the knot in his gut twisted and tightened. It was all inside. He had never released it; he did not know how. Closing his eyes, he tried to block out the gruesome sights. Somewhere, from far off, a voice brought him back to the present.

"Where's the major?" Barrett asked quietly.

"Don't know," the sergeant shrugged. He looked distantly removed from the others. Then, suddenly, he cracked. "But if they get him—you can all rot in Hell!" He dropped his head in utter emotional exhaustion. His shoulders constricted, as he struggled to control himself. A dry, despairing heave escaped his clenched lips, as the memories clamored for release. He could not let go. He was almost afraid that if he allowed any outpouring of emotion, it would run rampant until there was nothing left of him but a shell.

The fears that the Caves had wrought slowly wormed back into their consciousness. They had filled their bellies, yet something began to eat at them again.

"I never thought I'd ever hear that saddle-sore old pro cry," Gabe whispered softly. No one answered. No one had heard him.

Abruptly, as if passing through a door, the major came out of the dark. The camp as a whole breathed easy. "Well, we got one of them for a change!" he shouted as he approached. Behind him, half stumbling, half being dragged was the warrior, Taza. The major's belt was tied around the Apache's hands. Taza bled from his mouth and several cuts on his face. He was filthy beyond belief. His coat was covered with dried blood from old wounds, as well as new ones. He had put up a vicious fight and wore the marks of it. But he was badly bruised and beaten.

Talbot could not hide his deep relief at seeing the major. He and Gabe grabbed Taza. They forced him to the ground by using the Indian's arm as a lever. They jerked his arms up, high behind his back. Gabe quickly tied his wrists. The sergeant coiled the ropes rapidly around his feet. Then they roughly pulled arms and legs together. Taza twisted like a wild steer.

"That's Taza," the major nodded toward the beaten warrior. "Too bad I didn't get Naiche or White Horse. Or Geronimo, but, I goddamn well will!"

"This one isn't worth a nickel except to me. Geronimo's worth twenty thousand on the barrel." He inspected the thick scalp.

The major sat, hat in hand, breathing heavily. "It was hellish and horrifying. I'm half dead."

Gabe went to the fire, picked up a hunk of meat. Forgetting, he offered it to the major. "Like some meat? There's plenty meat for everybody."

"Meat?" The major turned. He looked at the fire, suddenly sick when he saw the gruesome remains of his horse. Grabbing one end of the spit, he jerked it up. It plummeted into the dark, carrying with it the shank of his animal. He looked over the rest of the butchered carcass. The sight brought waves of nausea rolling over his battered senses. He grabbed his pistol out of its holster. "I'm a man of my word. I meant it when I warned you never to touch my animal!"

"Major," Talbot said slowly. He knew the look in the major's eye and moved with utmost caution.

"Stay out of this, Talbot!"

"The horse was dead!" Venable said hesitantly, "You wanted it to rot?"

"We been half-crazed with hunger!" His wet lips crawled through his unruly beard.

Examining each man as though seeing him for the first time, he saw that they reeked of gloom and despair. They were haggard and wasted, worn like flapping soles of a shoe. All were visibly relieved as he turned away from them. He could not stomach their misery. There was no solace to be found in anger or mourning. His pain was not in his belly. It could not be touched, only felt. He searched for a reprieve, but found none. He felt as if he were alive at his own funeral, staring into his own grave.

Shaking himself away from his sinking thoughts, he asked, "Dull Knife get back?"

"He's out there still, Major."

"Then they got him?" Gabe's face was furrowed. He alternately stared at the major and the dark, not convinced that the horse incident had been settled. A man of his word seldom went back on it.

"Or," Venable said, "he deserted."

"I tell you this," the major leaned against the wall, "if they got him—they'll do him proper. For sure."

"Torture?" Barrett asked with a grimace.

"That don't half describe it. They'll cut him like calf

146

slobbers." He turned to Taza. "And that's what we're going to have to do to this one to make him show us the way out of here!" The major's face was as cold and impassive as the dead caves around them. Barrett shivered unwillingly as he saw the look in Pilcher's eyes. He shuddered at the revenge which boiled in the man. It was not natural, foreign to all that Barrett knew or believed in. But then, what was natural in these godforsaken caves?

The reporter's mind would have been further jolted if he had been able to see beyond the consuming black in the Caves. . . .

Far off in the caverns, in a place the party had not yet discovered, the Apaches followed their traditions. Dull Knife had joined them unwillingly. A searing knife wound in the shoulder was proof of that. But now, the wound was nothing. It hurt as much as a torn fingernail. His entire body was a gaping sore. Along a flat expanse, Naiche galloped his pony. In his hand was a rawhide rope. At the other end of the rope was Dull Knife's neck. The Apache's face was grim as he dragged the scout behind him. He took no pleasure in torture. Brutality was a thing he had learned from the white man. The Apaches lived by their wits. They used what their enemies used. The major had Taza. They had Dull Knife. They were doing only what the white officer would do. Geronimo looked on. He watched as Dull Knife's body was ground into one massive, bloodied bruise. There was no emotion in his face. Even the half-breed's silence did not turn his head. He stared as one does into a fire. He waited with the patience of generations.

Dull Knife's senses reeled but he pressed inward with his mind, with all his mental strength, as if he were trying to push his eternal spirit out of his physical body. He remembered the way animals died. They flashed through his mind, the raging of birds and rabbits. When beheaded and gutted, they ran blindly shrieking. No, he would not go like a rabbit. He remembered the cougar who with arrows cutting through him turned from the fight and ran, bravely on and on, finally slowing, then, almost at once, died. And never a shriek or a cry from his mouth. He would go like the cougar, not the jackal. He would suffer like the mountain lion, not bleat like the mountain goat. Soon he was beginning to feel his own animal spirit leave his body. It raced out of him and up, up into the stars. There he would stay. They would always have to look up to him, there, in the stars.

"That poor scout's probably getting a necktie party—Apache style," the sergeant whispered.

"While we sit here calm as toads." The sound of his own voice made Venable edgy.

Barrett half rose. "Makes me sick to my stomach."

The major ignored him, looked at Taza. "Now, then—it's time we made our Apache talk."

"Just because they torture. . . ."

The major warned, "Joshua, you go sit over there—and don't listen or look!"

"This is 1884, Major—not 1840!"

The major walked over to him. "It isn't issues at stake here, Barrett." He could see that he was not getting through. "It's lives. Ours—or theirs."

"Makes me sad that I have to stand helpless and let grown men act like animals." He stood, taunted them. "The only good Indian is a dead one, right, Gabe? Just what they always said about niggers." Raised in a nation of bigots, Barrett struck out at them in the only way he knew—through words. His reputation as a Lincoln liberal had cost him many jobs. But his beliefs were solid, his passion deep.

"And Jews," Gabe straightened up. "I ought to know!"

Venable eyed him derisively. "You a Hebe?"

Gabe flared his chest proudly like a mating pheasant. "My momma was."

148

"Don't believe it." For the moment, Venable relaxed from his watch. The only Jews he had ever seen were tight-assed shopkeepers in the cities. Jews were about as welcome in the West as Apaches.

"No?" Gabe looked him squarely in the eye. "Gabriel in the Bible was a Jew same as me. I play a Jew's harp, don't I? That's a dead giveaway!"

"Prove it." Venable's face leaned closer to him. "Let's see your pecker."

"You'll have to kill me first!"

The major's preoccupation had caused him to miss the exchange. He had been studying Taza. "Venable, Gabe!" They stepped back from each other. "Keep a lookout in case the Apaches try to rescue the prisoner. Me and Talbot will try to get this Apache to loosen up his tongue." With deference, he bowed slightly to Barrett. "In the nicest possible way."

The major knelt over Taza. "He's tricky, Talbot."

The sergeant sat back on a rock. Gun pointed right up against the Apache's head, he cocked it. Taza's eyes apprehensively moved back and forth between the two.

Barrett shuffled over to them, limping badly. Blood oozed with every step. His legs were immune to the pain, he was so incensed by the spectacle before him.

"An eye for an eye, Mr. Barrett," Major Pilcher said. "Go check the good book."

"And a life for a life? A war for a war?" The words tumbled out with all the compressed disillusionment of the sensitive trapped in an insensitive world. "That's what's always been wrong with this damn, stinking world we live in!"

"Well, you're the one that wants to change it!" Barrett's sincerity added fuel to the major's doubts. His raving convinced them all that he had surely succumbed to the insanity of the Caves. "You solve the world's problems, Mr. Barrett, I'll solve the West's!"

"You're taking advantage of a dumb savage!"

"Dumb!" the major exploded. "I'll tell you something about Indians, friend." Barrett stared at

149

him stupidly. "After they killed Mangus Coloradas, they cut off his head and sent it to the Smithsonian Institute in Washington—took out his brain, measured and weighed it." His voice grew in pitch and vexation. "It was bigger than Daniel Webster's!" he shouted. Barrett backed slightly away. "If you don't believe me, go to Washington and see it—it's still there!"

Barrett opened his mouth, was about to defend his position, if need be to the verbal death. But suddenly all eyes turned to the black void around them—to the sound of running. The sound jumped closer, almost on top of them. Then, suddenly, abruptly, it stopped. For a long moment, only the noise of their hammers clicking into firing position split through the dark. Then, the low, eerie roll of drums came again. Taza struggled against his ropes twisting wildly.

"Something's out there," Venable whispered.

Sergeant Talbot roughly pulled the Apache down, until his tongue lapped against the cold, stone floor. "They've come for him!" He cocked his pistol and held Taza still by the hair. The Indian froze as he felt the steel muzzle forced—right into his mouth.

Suddenly, something was lobbed over the wall. Venable instinctively shot. His hands trembled, his face paled. The object landed in the center of them. "Christ!" the major held it up. It was bloody. It was gory. "Dull Knife." It was the top of Dull Knife's head. He whirled around and shoved the oozing pulp of hair into Barrett's face. Barrett could not take his gaze off of the ghoulish sight. "What in God's name does it take to convince you, man!" Then, he flung the scalp in Barrett's arms. Barrett jumped back trying to disengage himself from the mangled web of hair and blood. It slid off of him and fell to his feet.

The major furiously jerked Taza to his feet and threw him over his shoulder like a sack of potatoes. Hardly noticing the weight, he carried him off into the dark behind them. The sergeant did not follow. The bloody heap at Barrett's feet made him nauseous. He felt faint and wavered where he stood. Gabe, unmoved by anything the Apaches could do, simply went about his business. He brushed Barrett aside and picked up the scalp. Slapping the scalp against the stone wall, he dislodged some dirt and blood. Then as casually as he would roll a cigarette, he tied it to his belt.

From the dark, inaudible Apache words were heard. Each time the major thudded his fist into the Apache, Taza opened his eyes and weakly smiled. Then he uttered the Apache word for *harder*. Each time the major asked him the way out, the Apache's voice—growing softer with each blow—answered with *harder*. . . .

Barrett shuddered with each blow. He clamped his hands over his ears. But the sounds crashed against his eardrums. Then it suddenly became unearthly quiet. Their bodies strained to hear. The major came back, breathing hard. His eyes held the look of retribution fulfilled. No one spoke.

The tunnel was close to forty-feet deep. The soldiers clawed at the rocks, like ants. Hoisting and passing their loads from scabby, blistered arm to arm. Their faces were black. Their eyes rimmed red. What was left of their uniforms barely covered their caked skin. Two soldiers patrolled. Their exhausted footsteps seemed to match the steady rhythm of the chipping from inside. Their heads lolled and bounced as they walked. Their rifles were draped over their arms, like baskets of bread.

High above them, eyes watched. The Apache Wolf, his face streaked in paint, stared down. The cavalry seemed to be no threat to him. Their condition weakened by the hour. The time was coming rapidly when they would feel his bite again. . . .

Chapter Fourteen

How long can a body hang upside down?" Barrett glanced toward the shadows.

"Half a day, maybe a day." The major took one last drag on his cheroot. He carefully extinguished it with his calloused thumb. It was the last one. He allowed himself a couple of puffs after eating. He, too, had finally relented and had eaten from his own horse. The meat had been sweet, a little stringy, no doubt from age. As each morsel had passed into his mouth, he had felt a further severing with his past. Each swallow had cleaved and burned his throat like unrequited hopes singe a man's soul.

"What if he dies?" Barrett was fused to the wall like a pile of dried, hardened rags. No one answered. He had not been able to keep the horse meat down. His body was wracked with fever. He was weak from vomiting. But his eyes worried him even more. A constant throb pulsated behind them, as if his body were trying to push them out. Bracing his elbows on his knees, he cupped his eyes with his hands. Sweat poured from his palms. In his daze, he thought it was blood.

The major stared at him, thought that if he did not snap out of whatever was plaguing him, they would soon have to carry him. He wondered if anyone would.

Gabe idly strummed his harp. It vibrated bizarrely. Its echoes were like ghostly whispers. He started singing, "There is no horse that can't be rode. There is no man that can't be throwed. . . ." Another sound came into the camp. Taza's moans had become louder, the tortured strains of his voice more wracked.

Almost as if to drown out the inhuman wails, Barrett

pulled out of his daze. "Why is Geronimo so bitter? So full of hell and hate?"

"It all goes back to when the Mexicans killed Geronimo's first wife, Alope, and his mother and three kids," the major answered with emotion. "For no reason at all." A cruel and senseless act had once been committed against the old warrior. His bitter years of revenge had been a natural consequence. But, Geronimo had carried it beyond all sane limits. No man—red or white—could be blamed for destroying the murderers of his family. But, in Geronimo's eyes, an entire race bore the guilt. One man's fury had changed the face of the West.

"Then, there was this John Ward business." Barrett looked confused. "Ward lost his son, Micky Free, to the Apaches. Boy grew up with 'em, wouldn't come back. Ward hunted him for years—riled up half the country. Helped massacre hundreds of Apaches and still didn't get the lad back." Barrett found his notebook and had begun to write furiously, even though he could barely see the page. It was all grist for his mill, the waterwheel of his reporter's mind slowly began to creak into use again.

"Ward?" Venable thought for a moment. "I remember him. Tall fellow. Had a twisted look on his face."

"Apaches get angry over the strangest things," the major's eyes were tinged with concern. "Like when we made them stop beating their wives and drinking tiswin—and cutting off the tips of their squaws' noses."

"Jesus! Why?"

"Tell Barrett, Gabe."

"That's Apache law for a squaw that took up with a white man." Gabe added sarcastically, "They should've just shot their wives dead like we white men do!"

Suddenly, from the dark, a great moan of agony rose followed by frantic Apache curses. The major listened, then wearily stood up. "I think Taza's ready to talk now. . . ." He moved off with stiff, lumbering steps.

153

The waiting, the sitting still, had made him feel just how tired he really was. The others stared anxiously at the place where he had vanished into the shadows. Then, he reappeared. Taza was hanging over his shoulder like a slaughtered lamb. The major dropped the Apache heavily. He landed with a thud, and rolled up protectively waiting to be kicked. His eyes narrowed like a cornered fox. The major knelt next to him, leaned close to listen. The Apache haltingly began to whisper softly in the major's ear. All the time, his eyes fearfully darted at all their faces. The major nodded and listened.

Somewhere another's ear listened. Not to words of betrayal, but to the quiet sounds of the Caves. His ebony eyes gazed into the red embers of a small fire. Geronimo sat beside it on crossed knees. His rifle was in his hands. It had become part of him like another limb. Naiche watched him as he cleaned a rifle. Before him was a pile of small arms, U.S. Government-issued carbines and pistols.

Geronimo was the fourth son of his father. He had four sisters, had four full-blooded Bedonkohe Apache wives and four mixed-blood Apache wives. Four of his children had been killed in the wars. Four were prisoners of the white government. His belief in destiny was entwined with the number four. He had come to the Caves with four. Now, one leg of the number had been broken. The wily officer had claimed Taza. Geronimo stared into the flames, trying to see what the destiny of three would bring. . . .

"Untie his arms, Sergeant." Taza had finished. The major nodded to the Indian and rose. "Gabe, give him a bit of that meat."

Gabe offered it. The Apache stonily refused it, keeping his mouth clenched shut.

"Well, what did he *say*, Major?" Talbot jerked the Apache around roughly and untied his arms. He quickly looped the rope around Taza's wrists, so that his hands would still be bound, but so that he would be able to move them slightly.

"We made a deal. He agreed to talk."

"In exchange for what?" Barrett asked cynically. "His life?"

"No. His death."

"His *death?*" Barrett thought he must have heard wrong. Everything was becoming a blur. Nothing seemed to make sense anymore.

"I had to promise to kill him." Then the major added, "I think we should lie and let him live. He'd never forgive me for that."

"What else, Major?" The sergeant slapped the rope that was tied to Taza against his palm nervously.

"He said that after White Horse made the avalanche, sealing us in—he joined the main body of Apache warriors," the major cleared his throat which had constricted with irony.

"Then?" Talbot asked apprehensively, almost afraid to hear the rest.

"Then while we were in here, they rode back to Fort Huachuca and burned the whole goddamn place to the ground!"

The sergeant's face drained.

"When the troops saw over seventy Apaches coming, they did the only thing possible—they deserted!"

"All?"

"Yes." The two soldiers stared at each other wondering if any had survived. To lose the fort would have been a major setback. There would be hell to pay for it. Washington would make sure of that. But, an entire company wiped out—they hoped to God it had not happened.

"Where's White Horse now?"

The major turned to Venable and shook his head. "God knows. My guess is he's come back to the Caves."

"Is he going to lead us out of here or not?" The news of the fort grated on the sergeant like sand. It had been his home for more years than he could remember. Like a man running into a burning house, he had to get back there—to see for himself.

The note of acrid chagrin unsettled them all. "He says—he doesn't *know* the way out. Only Geronimo does. . . ."

"He's lying." Gabe jumped up, ready to cut the truth out of the Apache.

"But he's sticking to his story." Taza motioned to the major who knelt beside him. The Indian muttered something in Apache. His face was grave. It was obvious he was begging.

"He wants to know," the major smiled wryly, "if we could kill him now?"

They had learned all they could from their prisoner. Further torture would do no good. Taza had already said too much. He preferred to die by a white hand than by a red. Reluctantly, the small group of men made ready to push on. As they gathered their meager provisions together, the major and the sergeant fulfilled their promise to Gatewood. They laid the corporal to rest under a tomb of stones. The others joined them and watched silently as the major placed Gatewood's dog tags and cap on a small wooden cross at the top of the grave. All were silent, heads bowed, hats clutched in their hands.

"Corporal Gatewood's bedded down now." The major gazed at the pile of rocks. "I guess he's been sent to Heaven to hunt for his harp."

"A harp is better than a gun, anyway," Barrett added.

"Well, let's just say," the major went on, "he sacked his saddle and rode upstairs. That's the way it is in this country. Out here if your life is the slightest use to anyone, be sure they will take it." He slapped on his hat and moved off. Taza struggled behind, his arms and ankles tied. The sergeant led him like a wild dog, with a rope around his neck.

White Horse skirted the lip of the cliff on his hands and knees. The legs of the wolf hide flapped against his sides as he crawled over to a ledge. Far below, two were sitting near the campfire. Occasionally, their eyes scanned the surface of the canyon. They seldom looked to the wall behind them. There had been no sign of Apaches for weeks. The absence of trouble had made them slack in their patrol.

The Apache slipped behind a huge boulder. A few feet next to it was a large indentation in the earth. The ground there had been recently disturbed. Lying in the hollow were slats of wood. White Horse gathered up the pieces. Placing one parallel to the boulder, he slowly began wedging the other under the stone. Now that the soldiers—most of them, at least—were inside the cave again, he could work leisurely, positioning the new fulcrum—preparing another even more ironic avalanche.

The dangerous dark was all around them. It was as cruel as the high noon sun on the desert. Gatewood, the bones of the major's horse, had been left far behind. All sense of time had been lost. There was no night or day in the Caves. They could not tell if they had walked for weeks or months. Their stomachs could have been some measure of time. But their bellies never ceased growling. All semblance of order had disappeared. They staggered through the dark, using only one torch. Its light was the only glimmer of reality around them.

The sergeant and Venable stood guard over Taza in turns. They fought more to stay awake than keep wary of their enemies. The Indian was crouched on the ground, despondently staring at nothing. The putrid air was a constant irritation to their eyes, which were swollen, puffed, slits. Thick vapor clung to the air. It rose from a hot, steamy pool. They sweated profusely. Their own stench was revolting.

"Hurry up, Gabe. It's my turn!" Venable shouted. The major, Gabe, and Barrett were all naked and bathing in the pool. Their weakness had had been momentarily forgotten. They splashed and dove in the hot, soothing water, blissfully, boisterously.

"In a minute!" Gabe barked. He was scouring his gritty hide with mud. Sighing with pleasure, he let the wet warmth glide over him. Barrett pounded his filthy coat against the rocks. He had scrubbed his pants so much that his knuckles were raw and pants threadbare. He psychotically rinsed and washed all the dirt and blood from the memory of his once-natty suit.

The sergeant suddenly stopped and moaned. "I'm dizzy—haven't eaten for over a day."

"And we won't all night, nor tomorrow either." The major stopped splashing. "We're out." They all reflected on this. Their mood changed. Again the worriment and sullenness became evident. The major pulled himself out of the pool, shook the water from his eyes. Pushing his eyebrows together with his fingers, he noticed how loose his skin had become. His belly was slack, empty folds hung on his arms and legs. He looked at the others—bony hunks of flesh.

Barrett pointed, "Over there—floating dead fish."

Gabe lunged through the water, half swimming. He picked one up. "Never saw a fish like this!"

"Pure white." The major took it and examined it closely. It was about fifteen inches long and weighed three or four pounds. He waded over to the torch. "And blind. Not just blind, *no* eyes!" Barrett stared at it curiously but did not touch it. It looked demonic, with smooth scales where its eyes should have been. It was so white it gleamed, in the dark.

"Let's eat it." Venable grabbed the fish from the major. It fell out of his overeager hands and onto Barrett's suit, which he had stretched out to dry. Barrett gingerly batted it away then washed his hands immediately.

"The thing that bothers me is—*what* killed it?" The major picked it up and turned the slimy cave fish in his hands.

Gabe took it from him and held it to his nose, sniffed it, recoiled from the pungent smell. "God! How long has it been dead?"

"I'll tell you what," the major now held the fish. "This cave killed it. When we've been in here as long as this fish—we'll be bleached white and just as blind." He dropped the fish into the pool. It floated lifelessly, weirdly, grotesquely. They all stared. Then, the major added with a note of resignation, "And just as dead!"

Both Bull Whacker and the judge looked like tired, old men. They had easily aged twenty years.

"No more food!" Tasker coughed, spitting up blood. He looked at the reddish phlegm in his hand, wiped it off on his pants.

"None?" Bull Whacker growled accusingly.

"Nope. Not even bone soup." They had not let one bit of Fly's body go to waste. For days they had been drinking a grayish, foul-tasting brew of mashed bones. Now that was gone. They had that morning squabbled over licking the rusty iron pot in which it had boiled. The judge sat weakly next to the kettle, gazed stupidly down into the empty bottom.

"I'm starving weak." Bull Whacker clumsily reached for the big pot, knocking it over. Running his fingers along the inside, he pulled out his hand and sucked his fingers. There was nothing to taste, but his own skin. He had grown so accustomed to the peculiar flavor of human skin that he hardly noticed.

The judge pulled Bull Whacker's hand out of his mouth. Bull Whacker at once realized what he had been doing. He had drawn blood on one finger.

"We're vultures," the judge nodded, his mouth flapping loosely with little muscle control.

"Worst thing I ever did. I never did nothing so low and vile. I'll surely roast in Hell for this."

"Both of us."

"We be damned!" Bull Whacker looked about as if watching for the hand of the Lord to smite him down.

159

Scrambling to his feet and mortally afraid, he crawled back into the tunnel.

The judge followed. The strain was telling. Suddenly, the judge remembered something from his past. The words crystallized in his mind. *"Remember— Christ said, 'Eat of my body.' "*

Bull Whacker clutched his hand to his stomach. A sinister thought crossed his face. "And now—there's just the two of us, Tasker." The judge did not like the disturbed look in Bull Whacker's eye. He jammed the tripod leg between two tightly packed stones. The leg bent and snapped. It fell useless from his hands. Bull Whacker's eye glinted crazily as he looked over the judge's body in a new light. . . .

Chapter Fifteen

A multicolored, mineral-streaked pit had seemed as good a place as any to stop. It was easy to guard with only one open side. The sergeant had patrolled for most of the night—or day—whichever it was on the outside. Whenever he rested his body sagged unnaturally—as if death were pulling at him. He was afraid to sleep because he preferred his chances on his feet.

Gabe and the major had somehow caught a small, green, slimy snake and two warty lizards. There were no bats in the area. They had eaten the meat almost raw, too hungry to bear watching it roast. While the others rested, too tired to actually sleep, Venable lunatically began digging in the limestone bed. At first he had idly scraped the soft stone, for wont of anything better to do. Then intensely concentrating, he burrowed with his hands and a small pick.

"What you digging that craphole over here for, Venable?" Talbot yelled over at the fusty, withered prospector as he paced along the opening of the pit. No one else even bothered to look up. To do anything other than eat or walk was a waste of life-giving energy.

Venable ignored Talbot and continued digging. Suddenly he stopped. He scooped up a handful of amber-yellow dust, stared at it unbelieving. "Je-sus!" He began to shout deliriously. "Dust! Gold dust! I swear on my life!" The others jerked out of their unrestful slumber, stared at his commotion. "I ought to know. I've been prospecting thirty years. This hole is rich! It's a vein!" Beaming, he picked up small rocks, which were scattered in the pit, and shoved them into their unwanting hands. He pointed. "It runs clean through these walls!" He ran his hands along an uncommonly gold-hued streak. "Biggest find since California!" He was so intoxicated by his discovery that he floundered around the pit, like a one-winged moth.

No one was impressed. Barrett had risen painfully on one elbow. Venable's jubilation had not been enough to push him to full consciousness. Through a fog, he could hear the shouting, but it was of no consequence to him. All that mattered was to be sure he kept breathing. Barrett counted to himself between breaths, forcing himself to inhale deeply at the count of ten. He was confident that if he could keep that up everything else would fall into place. He was sure that the major would pull him to his feet when it was time to go. It felt the same whether he was moving or lying still.

The major got up with annoyance. Venable was loud enough to raise the dead or any Apache within a mile. "Well, good luck, Mr. Brown. You just lug out a couple tons of it, bless your little heart." Venable shrugged the major off and continued his scrounging.

"*If* we ever find a way out!" Gabe stealthily inspected the rocks. His eyes widened appreciatively as he appraised the find.

"Don't you understand?" Venable was not to be discouraged. "I been looking all my life for a lode like this. These rocks are damn near solid gold. This is real pay dirt!"

"See if you can dig up a ham sandwich next, Venable," the sergeant scoffed, "or some hash and eggs." He spit and kept patrolling. Gabe looked away, trying to seem disinterested.

"Well, the hell with all of you!" He spread his feet wide. "I'm claiming it. From this day on this is the Venable Brown Mine!"

Gabe's eyes narrowed. He shoved one of Venable's feet aside. "Your claim is on that side of the hole, this side's mine!"

Venable started filling every one of his pockets with small rocks, then bigger ones. Soon his pockets were bulging, ripping. He even tucked some in his shirt until it was full. It bulged front, side, and back. He eyed Gabe suspiciously as the wizened scalper stooped for some rocks and kicked him away with his foot.

Seeing the start of trouble, the major intervened, walked between the two. "We're moving on!" Gabe sullenly backed off. He went to his pack, hoisted it on his back with difficulty, and tied on his strings of scalps. Then he booted Barrett in the ass. Barrett's eyes rolled lamely, as he recoiled from the blow. He feebly started getting up.

"Major," Venable began to panic, "I can't leave. This is my mine! Christ!" Venable's obsession was not based on greed anymore or even a yearning for materialistic wealth—for what could an old man really need? The gold was a fever—a fragmented dream. The end of the dream was lost years ago in the means to achieve it. Gold was a color emblazed like a scar across his fevered brain. It had haunted him all his life and now seemed to be the only fulfillment. Ah, yes, years too late, perhaps, but no matter. Wasn't it always like that? The fulfillment in itself had lost all meaning by the time it occurred. The victor was age, the elusive fantasy came not at all or always far too late. The gods, in retribution, had decreed it so.

"Well, Mr. Brown, when you get your shaft built, we'll all come back and help you lug out your nuggets." He pushed Venable out of the pit. As he went, Venable picked up a few more rocks, cradling them in his arms.

The major pulled Barrett to his feet, guided him a few steps, until he picked up momentum. Then he left him to fend for himself.

The sergeant turned to get Taza. But the Indian was gone. The rope he had tied around a stalagmite looked as if it had been chewed off. It had. "Gone!"

Major Pilcher pushed past him. He stumbled ahead into the dark, rifle ready. The others followed afraid of being left. The search quickly became an exercise in futility. They would never find Taza in the black maze.

Too much time and energy had to be spent in just finding each other. The group could not split up, to do so would have been disaster. Keeping up, and not losing sight of one another was all they could manage in their condition.

"We lost him." The major stopped, facing the others with resignation. "He's on his way back to the others. And the sonofabitch never did show us the way out." Yet another thread of hope had been cut. The heavy noose of their fate lowered them, inch by inch, down into the depths of no return.

Without light or any means to make a fire, Taza made his way through the Caves with a keen, unwavering sense of direction. It was not true that Apaches could see in the dark. He was just as much at the mercy of the massive bowels of Geronimo's mountains as were the white men. His cunning, his advantage was in using the Caves—not abusing them. In the pitch and quiet, he listened for the bats. They were the key. Their ever-present cries would lead him back to familiar ground. He followed the sounds until he had arrived in a chamber aglitter with faint phosphorescent streaks. He then began to follow a path of well-placed, glowing rocks, pointing like arrows along the dank floors and passageways. Luck or magic had nothing to do with the Apache's trail through the mountains. A distinct ribbon of light guided those that knew the secret. . . .

They had no strength to remember, no strength to complain. Only the miserable dragging of their feet held their attention. The major led, torch in hand. The weight of the rag-wrapped flare pressed heavily on his aching arms. Its fumes washed over his face, making him light-headed. Stops were frequent. Any movement in the shadows, no matter how small had to be investigated. It could be food, it could be death. They looked more for lizards now than Apaches. Their rifles became a burden. The muzzles dragged on the stoney floor, clanging and scraping noisily. The echoes followed them, surrounded them until the steely din seemed to emanate from their souls. They pressed on not knowing where they walked, or how far. Only that they were on their feet and were moving mattered.

Barrett had learned the sound of the major's footsteps and turned to them for direction. Talbot had failed by losing Taza. The guilt put a rift between him and the major in his mind. He trailed like a hound banished from the pack. Gabe and Venable could not forget the Mother Lode. They stuck close to each other almost as if afraid that one would turn back and scoop up the treasures from the guts of the Caves.

Venable staggered and swayed drunkenly from the weight of his gold-streaked rocks. His arms were still loaded down as were his clothes. As he walked, smaller rocks cradled in his arms slipped away. Neither of them noticed.

"Tell you what else I saw signs of, Gabe," Venable whispered confidentially. "Oil." His eyes were blazing. "In that black water we passed. Black Gold. Bet there's a lake of it under us." A few more small stones fell out. Gabe said nothing, merely eyed him dubiously. "I tell you," Venable insisted, "I know what I'm talking about—oil." He glanced at Gabe, sizing up his reaction with crazed eyes. "And I'll cut you in on it."

Gabe's eyes were indeed interested. "That's good of you, Venable." Half kidding, he asked, "See anything else?"

"Yes, goddamnit." He stopped. "I wasn't going to tell no one, but now that I'm rich, I don't care." He whispered, "I saw veins of silver, too." Then, his ecstasy carried him away. His voice rose, crustily. "And remember those rusty streaks I pointed to? *Copper ore!*"

Gabe walked nervously. The madness in Venable's eyes startled Gabe. "How long did you say you've been prospecting?" he asked, trying to calm him down.

"Five years."

"Five? Yesterday you said thirty! Now, which is it?"

Venable said with a complete straight face, meaning every word of it. "I been a prospector five years, but I spent twenty-five looking for my mules!"

"You're getting crazier than a loon, Ven." Gabe quickly moved away from him as if his madness might be catching. Venable followed slightly confused by Gabe's reaction. His arms still cradled rocks as if he were carrying a baby.

Hours? Days? No one knew or cared. They trailed past an underground lake. It was incredibly large or were their eyes playing tricks again? It was black, abnormally black. But then, so was everything in the Caves. They held their guns before them now. The grating of metal on rock had nearly driven them all mad. They distrusted every sound, every shadow. They had become paranoid as well as skeletal. Walking dead. The only truth they could hold on to was the beating of their hearts. Everything else—man, beast or shadow—existed in the netherland of their hallucinations.

"You all think I'm mad, eh?" Venable stopped again. "See that cloud of vapor?" They all slowed down, looked at him fretfully. His voice echoed around them like the wings of many demons.

"What about it, Mr. Brown?" the major asked. His weight sagged like a settling derelict. He did not have the strength to combat Venable's foolishness.

Venable looked at each with a demented, superior air. "Gas!"

"Come on, Venable," Sergeant Talbot groaned. Everytime they stopped to listen to the madman, exhaustion tugged at his limbs like anchors being sucked into a mire. Movement, perpetual motion was the only thing that kept him from sinking under.

"Smell it!"

The major started walking again. The others began to move away as well.

"Okay," Venable shouted at their departing backs.

166

"I'll prove it!" Begrudgingly they came to a stop again. Before they knew what was happening, Venable dropped his rocks. He ripped a piece of cloth from his shirt and pulled out a match. Lighting it, he ignited the cloth and threw it over the lake. Before the cloth had hit the surface, a wave of fire swept across the lake. The flames skipped almost playfully. Venable smiled maniacally. They all stared in wonder. The lights reflected vividly in colors over their faces. They shielded their eyes from the unaccustomed glare.

"See?" Venable hollered over the roar of the blaze. "You thought I was mad!" He babbled as he danced along the edge of the hell-fire. "When I came west, I was poor as a churchmouse. And now, I'm rich. Rich as a King!"

"He's getting worse, Talbot." The major's face, lit by the unholy flames, was furrowed. "Raving!"

"Why don't you just shoot him?" Barrett asked simply. Venable's delirium had affected him. The dwarfish figure held him mesmerized. He was beginning to recall the string of dead left behind on their trail to nowhere. At the center of it all stood the major. Paranoia began to eat through Barrett's brain like maggots after his life.

Despite the slow, muffled banging which came through the tunnel, the judge slept. His snores could even be heard above the din. His back was against a wall, his arm partially covered his face. From under the crook of his elbow, one half-open eye stared out at Bull Whacker. His body screamed for sleep, but he dared not to. He had to feign sleep fearing for his life. God knows how long they had been playing this game. He stared at Bull's reposing form. Or was he really asleep? He closed his eye for a moment. It burned and itched from its perpetual guard.

Suddenly, Bull Whacker opened his one good eye. The bandaged one was permanently closed. Quietly he sat up. He pulled out a jagged, rusted knife from under his blankets. Then, crawling, as softly as possible, which was not very—he stealthily made his way to the judge. Each forward movement was an agony of slow motion. His knees were open scabs, raw and bleeding. His hands were shredded and filled with cutting slivers of stone. He dragged himself along, his intent clearly in his eye. As he drew closer, his mouth began to drool, long, dangling dollops of brownish saliva. He shivered in anticipation. How good it would be to feel meat— fresh meat—slide down his throat. He could taste it already.

Suddenly the judge bolted up. Bull Whacker fell back on his haunches. The judge's shoulders quaked, his eyes pierced him like an arrow. Slowly, Tasker pulled his arm into view. In his hand was a hatchet. Both breathed hard, their faces drenched with sweat. Their bony arms trembled, as they clutched their weapons until their marrow seemed to crumble. Like two animals, they faced each other, preparing for the kill. All humanity had vanished from them. Their backs were hunched like crippled jackals, their back hair standing on end. Like scorpions, their minds had been poisoned by the venom of starvation.

"We can't go on like this, Bull." The judge's breaths were coming shorter, raspier. "We can't work, can't sleep."

Bull Whacker's voice was lined with threat, but lacking pitiably in power. "I'm dying, man!"

"So am I." He dropped the hatchet a few inches. "But, it's no reason to do what we done to Fly to each other."

He let the weapon fall to his lap, but didn't let go of it.

"There's only ten, fifteen feet between us and them outside."

"That's two weeks more." Bull Whacker's lips twitched. "We'll be gone. I could barely move this morning."

"Me, neither." He could barely move now. Holding

Bull Whacker at bay was draining him completely.

"The pain," Bull Whacker slumped. His eye rolled and bobbed in his head. He clawed at his cheek, trying to dig out the source of his misery.

They were both too weak to kill. Bull Whacker seemed to have forgotten his aim. The confrontation was over. The judge recounted, "The Lord said suffer and be cleansed."

Suddenly, Bull Whacker bristled like a cactus. "How the hell would you know what the Lord said, you old fool?"

"You're wrong, Bull." He solemnly shook his head. "I never was a deacon, I admit. But, I was a judge." A wry smile parted his swollen, blistered white lips. "A crooked one, sure enough. But with my tongue, I could've been a senator instead of a fool."

"Why don't you just let me put you out of your misery, Tasker?" Again the demented gleam came into his one good eye. "I've killed six men in my life, one more would be lucky."

"For who?" he quipped. "Me or you?" The standoff began again. The two mad dogs just sat there. They watched each other like rattlesnakes each ready to strike. All the time the pounding came from outside. Closer, louder. It split their ears as though they were trapped inside a tremendous, beating drum. They had to let up, their muscles were too deteriorated to endure their death watch.

Chapter Sixteen

A clear, running pool beckoned them to stop. Towering above it were limestone pillars, which in the dim light almost looked like trees. It was cool, the air unusually fresh. The small party staggered to it. They collapsed on and over the cold rock edge. Sprawled, lying on their backs, they were shattered. Like shipwrecked hulks, they did not move. Their limbs were twisted where they had fallen, their legs and arms reaching out like roots. They gulped in the good air, drank long breaths of it.

The major was on his stomach, drinking from the pool. He held his lips to the water for a long time, sucking it into his mouth, his bloated eyes closed. Suddenly, she was there—Baby Doe, in his mind's mist—gossamer, diffused. She had begun to inhabit his daydreams as well as his night. The major sighed, something in him hurt in what was becoming an old ache.

He snapped his eyes open lest the dream should become real, and if it did, he would go mad.

For a long while only half their strained breathing and the sound of gentle trickling could be heard. "If those two Apaches show now," the major's voice came back, soft, sluggish, "they'd kill us for sure." The others looked up without expression. "We couldn't do a thing." There was no light of hope in any eye.

"Haven't seen a sign of them for weeks," the sergeant huskily whispered. Their time had been spent mostly groveling for food, hours crawling like insects themselves, slapping desperately in the dark after quickfooted lizards and bugs. Bugs and worms, spiders and ticks. They had given up on bats, which were impossible to catch anymore.

"How long have we been in these Caves?" Barrett asked. "Lost all track—of time. A month?"

"More," the major stared off. "Much more. . . ."

"Two months?" His voice was high pitched, laced with hysteria.

"I know why those Apaches haven't attacked."

Gabe stared at the sergeant with dull, lifeless eyes that peered out from permanent pockets of water. "Why?"

"Because they left."

"That could be." Major Pilcher had guessed that days ago. He had not said anything, because fear of the Apaches was one thing which had kept them going, alive.

"They left," Venable sat up, "and sealed up the other way out, too!"

"Then," a resigned tremor crawled through the sergeant's words, "we're finished. Amen!"

"You don't know that, Venable, so shut your mouth!" The major spoke sharply.

"Then how come we can't find it?" Venable said accusingly. "How come we're going around and around in circles?"

"What are you talking about?" Gabe questioned, looking nearly as crazed as the prospector.

"Did we," Venable started slowly, "or did we not," he pointed, "pass this underground stream—these same rocks—*three* times?"

"No, goddamnit. Twice!" A gulf of despair came into the major's face. It was a good ten minutes before anyone spoke again. Barrett smiled inwardly at the cruel irony of it all. Circles. They had been walking around and down into the circles of Hell. He wondered what level they reached. How much further they had to go until they came upon their assigned ring in the Inferno.

"We must be in Mexico by now!" Gabe's ear was

pressed to the rock listening, his eyes wide.

"How do you know?" the sergeant perked up.

"Because, I think I hear Spanish music."

"Major," the sergeant leaned closer, "I think we got another nut on our hands."

"Sure, you have," Gabe grinned. "Me and you and Venable and the major. We're all mad now!"

Deep in the tunnel, the lieutenant slammed his pick against the far wall. The sound was not the usual dim thud. It was sharper, more resilient, as though air was behind the rocks. He hit it again.

"Hollow!" Orley shouted excitedly back down the line.

"Must be less than two feet to go!" Hicks scrambled up next to him. Their faces, though drawn and worn out, gleamed with the knowledge that they were almost there.

The lieutenant shouted until his lungs were bursting, "Hello!! Hello!!"

The sergeant's, Gabe's, and Venable's depression was so deep-rooted they could not move. Barrett, sick as he was, painfully wrote in one of his notebooks. Each word took a minute. The major, boots and hat off, shirt open, sat at the edge of the pool.

Gabe's eyes were downcast as was his spirit. "I haven't got the strength to move one toe let alone a foot."

The sergeant said with little emotion. "This is as good a spot as any to go to glory."

"At least we won't die of thirst."

"I'm not dying," Venable spoke up. "I have too much to live for!"

"What are you writing, Barrett?" Talbot asked. "If you're writing your last will and testament, I'll be pleased to witness it."

"I already wrote my will."

The major looked at him with concern. He doubted

that Barrett would last much longer. "I left my estate to Mr. Fly."

They doubted if Fly would ever collect. If he would, then they had made a mistake that would surely cost them their lives.

"What are you writing now?"

"I'm writing our story," Barrett replied. "So, at least, if they ever find us the world will know."

They quickly lost interest in Barrett. It was a fool's notion to think anybody would ever find his notebooks at all. The only ones that knew where they were were the Apaches—and Apaches did not read.

Seeing something, the major reached down into a crevice by the pool. "Look, here!" He pulled out a small leather, crudely decorated bag. They all stared, then crawled over—even Barrett.

"What the devil is it, Major?"

"It's an old Apache rawhide pouch." He turned it in his hands and studied it. "For medicine or luck beads." He held it upside down and shook it. "Nothing in it, now."

"But," Gabe asked, "what's it doing here?" A nervous rush went through them.

"Don't know." The major's face lit up. "But that tells us one thing, for sure. The Apaches came this far. They were definitely here. Sitting on this very rock, the same as us."

"But then what?" Barrett gazed at the pouch dangling in the major's hand. Its rocking motion hypnotized him.

The major studied the water, trying to work something out. "I'm not sure," he mumbled, distractedly.

"What's going on in your brain, Major?" The sergeant crept next to him.

"This stream leads underground." He dipped his hand into the water. The current was strong. "But, how far?" To where?"

Venable and Barrett, mouths drooping open, tried

hard to follow the conversation.

"It *must* come up somewhere!"

The sergeant looked up. "In Mexico?"

Suddenly, Venable became excited. "It don't god-damn matter to me *where* it comes up," he jabbered, "only *if* it does!" Barrett did not comprehend the gist of their rapid words. He continued to stare at the pouch like a fish at a worm.

The major tore off his shirt with fumbling hands. "Well, I'm going to find out!" With that, he dove—feet first—heavily into the pool. They all peered down after him.

At first he let the current carry him. He drifted underwater with eyes open, hair streaming behind. Quickly he came up against solid rock. He followed it down until he found a crack in the wall. It was too small for a body to get through. Remembering a saying from his childhood, he turned and swam against the rushing water. Upstream was always harder, but it got you there. The bottom of the pool was a garden of colors. A school of small fish scattered as he pushed on. The water seemed to shimmer and glisten, change moodily, mistily, eerily.

Suddenly, he realized why and lunged, gasping in his breath, toward a sparkling shaft of sunlight. He approached, dying for air, fighting not to gulp water. Then, he reached it. Coming straight down through the water was a beam of soft light. Treading water, he gazed up into an old well. He could hardly believe what he was seeing.

Hanging from the old, rotting timbers along the base of the well was a long slimy green rope. He grabbed it, his fingers sliding down the moss-encrusted hemp. The rope went down, as well as up. Up from the pool. He had found the way—the real way out. He had beaten the old warrior at his game. He felt like kissing the rope. It was surely a lifeline. He glanced once more quickly up the well, then turned back. He soon found the rope had been tied around several elongated rocks in several places along the underwater channel that led back. Pulling and swimming, lungs almost bursting, he returned once more to the Caves.

He surfaced, clutching the end of the rope for life. Clinging to the low, flat rocks he drew in great heaving gulps of air. One after another. Sharp, rasping jolts. The others stared at him. Expecting the worst of their fears. Cushioning themselves against failure.

"What did you find, Major?"

He did his best to get the words out between gasps, "The stream is long—seems to go up. There are air pockets, along the rocks—about one hundred feet on, I can see. . ." he coughed and gagged, "daylight!"

"Daylight?" Talbot, barely able to contain himself, shouted, "From where?"

The major choked and sputtered. "The sun—down some sort of shaft—like a well!"

"A well!"

"A well." The major's breath was steadier now. "Hanging from it was this old rope."

Venable, who had been listening with increasing confusion, echoed, "Rope?"

The sergeant helped pull the water-logged major out of the water. Strangely, neither men felt anywhere as weak as they had minutes before. The major held the slimy green hemp. "Just what the Apaches could have used to go up." He bit his lips. "Well, I'm going back—and *up!*"

"I'm game," came from the sergeant.

"The rest of you?" Vacant, bewildered eyes gazed back at him.

"I can't," Barrett's voice was shaking. His eyes dull, lifeless. His whole body, one throbbing pain. He held his thick notebooks tightly against his chest and looked at the green-blue water. "My notes. . . ."

"Bring your head, Mr. Barrett—it's got your notes in it, doesn't it?" The major was beyond patience and did not try to conceal his exhilaration. "As far as I can see. It's this—or the deep. Make up your minds—which is it to be?" Venable's face became perplexed. Gabe's mind whirled.

"We can all just follow that rope." Talbot had already made up his mind. He voiced the thought to help convince the others. "And me."

They all reflected on this.

"I don't know if I got the strength left," Gabe sighed.

"Find it!" pressed the major.

"I want to go," Venable stammered, "but I don't know if I can swim that good—or far."

"We'll never get through," Barrett began to panic. "We'll drown."

"Here, we've had it. I promise you that."

Venable's eyes brightened. "It's a good chance. We got to take it!"

"I'll lead—just do what I do—swim like a fish."

"Can we breathe like a fish, too?" Gabe asked caustically.

"If anyone wants to stay behind, I won't stop them." The major searched their faces. "I don't know any other way—except dying. Beyond any doubt, we've stumbled on Geronimo's way out!"

The sergeant began to take off his shirt. Then he quickly slipped into the water. Clinging to the rocks with one arm he waited. On seeing this, Barrett, mindlessly, in a frenzy began to disrobe. He could not be left behind; they would not wait for him. He had always managed to keep up. More by force of habit than conscious will he dropped into the water next to the sergeant. He still held his notebooks. The water quickly saturated them. A small trickle of black ink ran down his chest and was carried off by the current. Gabe slowly unbuttoned his shirt, still not entirely convinced. He would make up his mind in a minute. He stumbled back to his gear and began strapping on his strings of scalps. Water would not hurt them. Wet or dry, they were still worth a hundred silver dollars each.

"Hurry, Venable!" Major Pilcher waited at the edge of the pool.

"Well, I thought. . . ." He stopped.

"Je—sus! The man's bulging all over with gold rocks!" Talbot yelled incredulously.

"They're too heavy." The major pulled out several four- and five-inch round stones from Venable's shirt. "They'll drag you down, man!"

"But I'm taking them—or I'm not going!"

"That's greed for you! Take *half!*"

Venable took out a few more rocks. He reached to pull out another, then changed his mind. "That's it. I'm taking all the rest!"

Shaking his head, the major dropped away, down, disappearing under the water, following the rope. Barrett fearfully ducked under, clinging behind him, followed by the sergeant.

Old Gabe, still on the surface, picked up one of Venable's rocks. "All my life, I've been sweating for scalps—and got nothing to show for it." There was a dangerous glint in his eye. "I'm old as you. It's time I got a break. All I want is to share. Give me half!"

"Of *my* gold?"

"Damn you, Venable," Gabe's mouth twisted. "Give me half—or I'll take it!"

"Will you, Gabe?" Venable was ready for a fight. His inflamed eyes stared black. "Well, nobody's taking *my* gold. You'll have to fight me to the death, hear? You'll do it over my dead body!" With that, Gabe lunged for his throat and got it. Venable thrashed with his arms, trying to fight back, but the weight he was carrying stemmed him. The two men swayed and tottered. They fell together heavily onto the stone, groaning as they battled.

Rocks spilled from Venable. He found one and smashed it into Gabe's face, trying to break free of his grip. Gabe hung on to Venable's throat with all his strength. His thumbs were sunk deeply into the prospector's jugular vein. Both men had been pushed over the brink, their eyes maddened, snorting, hissing in battle. Venable tried desperately to unloosen Gabe's

177

death grip. His temples were pounding with unbearable pressure. His vision blurred and darkened. His eyes grew wide in terror as he felt himself lose hold. Venable's struggle lessened. Gabe tapped an unknown reservoir of strength and swung Venable viciously like a cat over the side into the pool. Venable immediately began to cry out, but his mouth quickly filled with water. He began to sink rapidly under the weight of his hoard, as if he were being sucked down. Gabe, gasping from the strain, watched. . . .

Suddenly, he snapped out of his fevered stare and cried out, "Venable!" But it was too late. Venable sank like an anchor plunging down and down. In one last desperate movement, Venable reached out for the trailing rope. It slipped greenly past his fingers, as elusive as life was for him now. Bubbles trailed from his open mouth. Helplessly, Gabe stared at the spot where Venable had gone down. Then, finding the rope, he filled his lungs and went after the others.

Their eyes were blinded. They swirled and paddled against the water that seemed to push them down. Their hands slipped and grasped along the rope, all the time desperately following the major. Cheeks bulging, they fought to hold their breaths. Barrett's mouth flew open for air. He coughed and sputtered, almost drowning. The sergeant pulled him on as he managed to recover. All around them like teeth were razor-sharp, jutting stones. The stones' dangerous edges protruded and scraped against them as if they were passing through the gigantic mouth of a swallowing sea monster.

Suddenly, eerily, the bloated, open-eyed corpse of Venable Brown thudded against the rope, drifting in slowed, strained motion. On his face was a strange smile, as if he knew some ironic joke that he would not tell. The major pointed. They all stared—their eyes grappling to see in the water—at the dead, floating corpse. Barrett opened his mouth to cry out. He struggled and thrashed but slowly regained control.

Venable was tossed limply into them by the currents. He was pushed away by several unnerved hands. Silently he floated off, perhaps to eternally work his claim in the depths of Hell. They moved on, trapped more than ever. For now, even their breath—their air—was held in the mocking fist of their unrelenting torturer, Geronimo's Caves.

Chapter
Seventeen

The judge was perched up on a rock, hatchet in hand, insanely guarding himself from his nightmare. Crouching like an ape, his blistered, lolling eyes followed Bull Whacker. They had given up working in the tunnel. Let the others come for them. Not one more rock would be lifted by either. Neither could trust the other enough to turn his back and crawl into the dead-end hole. They had done enough.

Bull Whacker gazed into the tunnel. If only they would stop that infernal pounding. He twitched as each hammering blow came from it. It was now loud, filling the cave like a cacophony of Doom. Each hour it came closer, all consuming, like the scourging lash of many tongues. It sounded grotesque and distorted in his mind. Desperately, he tried to shield himself from the Devil's roar.

"Stay away from me, Bull!"

Insanity washed over Bull Whacker's face. The sound of a voice had become alien to him. Speaking had taken too much out of them, so they had both stopped. The noise of the picks inside his head swelled and multiplied. He saw something—was it Fly? His hands groped spasmodically, wrestled with his belt, unwound it from his waist. It was his whip, which had been coiled several times around him. He grappled and tugged until it dangled freely in his quaking hands.

Bull's madness did not come all at once, although it seemed so to the judge. The strain, the nervous exhaustion added to the breakdown, but the seed had always been there. It was there in the beginning—in the lost child's eyes, but none noticed. Little things gave it away all his life. The mental collapse of men under great stress was only the end product, the filtering down of the dregs of a whole life. It was an escape, the way out—either that or Death. So his mind decided to shut off—build its own world. A totally new one, free of danger because it was too terrible for his poor, dim, brain to contain.

"What's that I hear?" He peered into the dark, toward the black hole—the mouth of the tunnel. "Who's coming for me?" He squinted. The judge strained, but he could not see what Bull did. Raising his long whip, he suddenly snapped it at the small black figure he was sure he saw. "Back! By God!"

"You're demented, Bull," the judge hollered, enraging him further, "stark, staring as a loon!"

Bull Whacker cracked the whip again over his head. Moving further off, he saw real Devils coming for him. "I see—horns, too—Satan's himself. Devils—all comin' for me. Back I say! Souls, bodies, and tails!" He cracked the whip loudly. "Jump, then! Condemnation overtake your ears, and your brandmarks!" His arms flayed. The whip snapped. "Evil One take you away!" The whip crackled and cracked, slicing through the air like lightning. "I'll drive you back into the fire!" He waved the whip madly before him. "Curse your tallow and hooves! Your hide! Your ribs and your knee-joints, and bones and everything else that ever wore horns! Your dewlaps and livers! Curse you from here to Hell!"

He turned, whirling, almost falling. Sweat literally poured off his face, saliva from his mouth. His head jerked around as if he saw the demons on all sides. He blinked and stared. Suddenly, the long dead figure of Fly loomed once again into his sight. Close, closer. The mutilated corpse began to come in anger now, nightmarish, slowly, menacingly toward him. One arm was missing. The chest was gouged and bloody. Bull Whacker gasped. He raised his whip protectively and struck out. But, the gruesome shadow did not stop.

In Bull's head, Fly had come back for his heart. It

steadily dragged closer and closer, until Bull Whacker could feel its cold, dead, stench of breath. Bull raised his arm to strike the whip again, but Fly lunged upon him. He grabbed Bull Whacker's arm and pulled it back with his one good hand, wrestled with all the strength of the dead. The judge slid down from his stony perch, staring at Bull Whacker's bizarre dance.

Bull Whacker grasped and fought only air. He struggled for his life with a figment of his own guilt. Suddenly, his whip flew from his hands, as if jerked away with the awesome power of death. He was tortured with a terrible fear. He groped for breath. Then his entire body began convulsing, a grimace contorted his face. He simply sat down on the cold, stone floor, his eye wide and staring. . . .

The major surfaced gratefully sucking in air. Clinging to the rocks, he scanned the tight, three-foot air pocket and crevice above him. To his starving lungs, the stale air tasted sweet. Seconds after, Barrett, the sergeant, and Gabe broke through the icy, blue water. They coughed and spit. Gulped in air. Their bodies trembled and bobbed in the water weightlessly like corks. The limestone was slick, hard to clutch.

"My ears is busting," the sergeant tried to rub his ears and hold on as well. He slipped under, came up sputtering. "My lungs. . . ." His chest was ripped with a raw, frigid sting.

Barrett's whole head was puffed. His eyes were nearly swollen shut. His skin had an unnatural bluish hue.

"Breathe deep!" the major gasped. Having swum the distance once already and back, he could barely support his own weight. All the time, the current was pulling at their legs, sucking them down. Back down into the Caves.

Gabe felt himself going. He clawed at the slimy rock ledge with bleeding fingernails. "Can't hold on. . . ." The major supported him with his shoulder propping him back against the rocks. Gabe reached out. "I'm sinking—" The major pushed him up until he was jackknifed over the edge. Gabe's chest scraped against the stone; he was slowly inching his way back down into the swirling waters.

"Venable?" The major's accusation was clearly in his tone. Something had been amiss with the floating, bizarre corpse that had crossed their watery path.

"Gone." Gabe looked away from them, guilt clearly in his face. "Gone—to his Maker."

"Where we're all going!" Barrett whispered. The fight was too hard, too much to ask of them. The odds were too great. Their time was nearly up. Even the major was ready to admit it, to give in, to sink into the sweet salvation of oblivion.

The sergeant also sensed that Gabe was hiding something. "How?"

"Drowned!" The major and the sergeant were beginning to guess the truth.

"He hung on to his gold—but not his life," Gabe muttered.

"Well, there's no going back," the major whispered hoarsely, looking at each torpid face, ". . . for any of us." A shudder went through them. "Just another half a hundred feet to the well! I swear!"

Suddenly, a loud cracking sound filled the small air pocket. They all jerked away from the ledge. All but Gabe. The rocks they slumped on began to rip apart, break away. The whole shelf sent a tumult of limestone dust and chippings down on them. The major's hands groped under the water for the rope. Barrett desperately reached out for a hand. He grabbed the major's kicking leg.

With one hand on the rope, the major reached down pulling Barrett by his coat, dragging him away from the falling stone. Barrett tossed and pitched wildly. The major hauled and lugged them both toward the glittering shaft of light. It could be seen in the distance like a mirage. Barrett's blinded eyes saw nothing but black. They struggled on fighting each other and choking in the swirling current.

The sergeant, momentarily stunned, began to follow. Rocks were falling all around him. He turned to see old Gabe gasping for breath, mouth open, beginning to drown. Several rocks thudded down on him. Without thinking, the sergeant lunged back. He held Gabe's panicked body. He struggled with the weight, the falling rocks, and the building suction of the undertow. For a moment—clinging together—the two bodies drifted back and down. Talbot looked off towards the wavering figures of the major and Barrett in the murky distance. He would not be left behind. He clutched Gabe to his chest, shaking free of the Cave's unyielding hold and moved toward the light.

The well was five feet in circumference. Thick, green algae lay over the surface of the water like a velvet blanket. The major's feet thudded and kicked against the rocky sides of the well. Up, scratching desperately up out of the water. Suddenly, he exploded through the surface. Barrett broke through seconds behind him. They choked, spewing out water, sucking in life. Blood pounded against their ears. Their lungs and eyes burned. The algae settled over their faces, their eyes, like a mask. Holding the rope and each other, they slowly, agonizingly, regained their equilibrium. The air was so clean and pure that their unaccustomed bodies reacted to it like smoke. They coughed uncontrollably, wheezing with each breath.

"Talbot," the major peered down into the distant, churning, cold well.

Seconds later, the sergeant emerged, still clutching the half-conscious Gabe. All were completely depleted. Exhaustion crushed their bodies. The major slumped his head against the cool rock with lingering, intangible solace. He held onto Barrett as he had held onto life. A bond as permanent as death sealed the men. Their differences, their fights meant nothing now. Their souls were fused with the awesome knowledge that they had walked together through Hell—and were barely alive.

Still gathering his strength and quelling his shattered emotions, the major looked up. His eyes painfully adjusted. He stared in disbelief, in wonder at the hot, baking sun—at the miraculously, azure sky. It was as if he was seeing it for the first time. As his sight filtered into focus, he could make out, circling, floating in air against the blue, black carrion crows.

The lieutenant, Orley, and Hicks all grappled at the heavy stone. Goddin was squeezed between them, the others behind in the tunnel reached out waiting to pass the stone down the line. Then Orley screamed, "I'm through!" The tunnel seemed to tremble.

Immediatety a putrid stench came rushing out at them. They flicked at their noses, as if to push the smell of stale air and gangrenous lives away. Wesley Bernard leaned down through the hole and called out into the dark. "Major!" He squinted into the black. "Major Pilcher!" But not a word was heard—only their own echoes came floating back in lonely reply.

Bracing themselves on the wet, slippery stone sides of the well, the major and Barrett slowly, awkwardly inched their way up. Behind them Talbot and a strangely subdued Gabe struggled. Their feet slid on the slimy sides, as they groped for footholds, lost ground, slipping back and slithered again. The climb was agonizing. Their arms seemed to be ripping out of the sockets. Their hands bled. Streaks of red smears and clumps of flesh covered the old, twisting, raw hemp, which they painfully pulled themselves up on, to an ancient, wooden, crossbar at the top of the well. If the wooden bar snapped, they would be finished. The well was filled with their groans of despair and grunts of hope. An occasional cracking sound bounced against the walls. They stared at the trembling and shuddering crossbar prayerfully. Their bodies hung together, supporting one another, their shoulders smashing together, their arms interlocked. Hand over hand, they clawed their way up.

As the sound of the crumbling wall—the song of their reprieve—had reached their distorted ears, Bull Whacker and the judge had drawn instinctively together. For the moment, their distrust and fear of each other had been set aside. The voice from outside, booming the damnable word *Major* had terrified them beyond all rational limits.

Slinking into the shadows, they cowered behind one of Fly's trunks. Trembling together, neither spoke, words far beyond their broken minds. They wished that they could slither between the crevices of stone, like lizards, and wait until the danger had passed. They hid from their rescuers, seeing damnation in salvation. No longer men, they had become creatures of the Caves.

The lieutenant pulled himself through the small, rough opening. Orley, Hicks, and Goddin slithered after. Then they crawled through the tunnel on the other side to its mouth. There, slowly, they stood and walked into the Caves. "Major!" the voice called again into the shadows. *"Major Pilcher!"* Nothing answered. Only the voice shot through the dank, damp cavern. Then it died. They stood for a moment, confused, afraid, disappointed. Their nostrils were seared by the overwhelming stench of decay. Their torchlight spread before them, glimmering into the corners, finally revealing two inhuman faces.

They stared in revulsion at the depraved, insane eyes of the judge. And at the grotesque hulk of Bull Whacker clinging to his side. A curdling chill swept through them. They could not take their eyes off the grotesque pair. They could not help but wonder if all those trapped inside had gone mad as well. Had they worked too slow? Could the putrefaction of these men's souls be their guilt?

The major was the first to reach the top. He hesitantly, wondrously, curiously stuck his head out. He looked slowly about blinking his blurred eyes in the dazzling sun. He did not speak.

"Where are we, Major?" Barrett, a few feet below him, called up, his voice muted and hollow.

"A churchyard." The major continued to stare, as he clung to the top of the wall. "Spanish. . . ."

"Any sign of Geronimo?"

The major looked around at the desolate area. His eyes scanned an ancient, broken, crumbling rock fence. Behind it was a dilapidated, old church. Further off—a graveyard, abandoned a century before. And on the ground—sprawled in front of an unhinged gate were two priests' bodies. Their crude wool robes were shredded. One's head lay in a pool of blood. He had no scalp. The other's hands were clasped, his knees bent forward, as if he had been praying or begging when the smattering of bullets that riddled his chest and face had cut him down. Both were stiff.

"Yes," the major muttered softly, with little expression or emotion. "Geronimo was here."

White Horse, in his wolf's skin, gazed down at the two soldiers who patrolled below him. He was perched on the rock ledge over the Caves' entrance. The lieutenant, some distance off, stood sheltered by a rock refuge. He unfolded a long telescope and held it in his hand. His face was grim. He stared at the Apache through the cracked lens, broken despite the leather case that held it at his side during the avalanche.

Suddenly, White Horse heard something behind him. He turned, moving to his feet. Four soldiers, rifles nervously raised, stood behind him in an arc on the ledge. White Horse's face, encased by the head of the wolf, gazed at them. Then without a sound, he turned and moved to the edge of the cliff. The soldiers stopped and watched him curiously. Standing solemnly, tall and straight, White Horse raised his arms skyward to the Sun God. His eyes glared, then softened. With the pain of innumerable defeats, he asked if his time had come. A grave, bitter smile came to his lips. Then, arms extended, he dove, birdlike, over the edge of the cliff.

Barrett, Gabe, and the sergeant were sprawled in the summer-bleached grass. They let the hot sun pour over them. Every pore of their bodies drank in its warmth.

The reporter's eyes welled up. "Never believed I'd ever see ground again!" He kissed the earth. "I gave up a dozen times, a hundred!" Shutting his eyes, he felt each muscle and bone let go of the dreadful weight of fear. They all seemed to be floating, at peace.

Major Pilcher walked slowly, hesitantly through the graveyard, past windbent and broken, crusted headstones. He moved quietly, reverently, felt no physical pain. It had all been left in the Caves. His body was ripped and torn, yet he felt nothing but an overwhelming, all-consuming relief. His eyes were moist and filled with emotion. Looking up, he shook his head in wonder. For the first time in months, he gave in totally to the simple, exquisite luxury of being alive.

Epilogue

Iron handcuffs and chains cut into Geronimo's wrists. His legs were shackled as well. Behind him and around him were decrepit shacks in various stages of decay. The ground was parched and cracked. There was little movement in the reservation. The years of burden were clearly evident on the old warrior's face. Yet, his eyes had not lost their glow of defiance. The White Man had not claimed that.

Sitting beside him was Joshua Barrett dressed in a clean, tweed suit. The air of middle-class respectability was once again on him. His wounds were healed. His eyes had mended though now he had a perpetual squint. In his hands was his eternal notebook. It was not as frayed as the ones he had left in the Caves, but it was battered and well used. As always he was making notes.

Across from him sat Major Emmett Pilcher. The clothes and the uniform were the same but he seemed somehow different. Perhaps it was the glasses. They caused a slight change but there was something more. His face was much older, mellowed, lined with deep furrows.

The letter from the president was still in Barrett's possession. The ink had run making it illegible, but the directive was etched in his mind. He had come west to record Geronimo's story for posterity. He had done just that.

The fort had been rebuilt. It was almost two years later that Geronimo surrendered with Naiche. Geronimo curiously chose to give himself up to the major personally who turned his prisoners over to General

Miles who had replaced General Crook.

The major translated; Barrett wrote: "Because you alone have always proved yourself a brave warrior worthy to accept my surrender." The major gazed at Geronimo for a long moment. Then Geronimo went on, "It was the greatest honor I could give you."

The general's orders had been simple and direct. The major was to escort Geronimo to a reservation near Tucson. Then he was to take his prisoner to a government compound far away from the Huachuca Mountains, Skeleton Canyon, and the Caves.

"Geronimo says," the major translated for Barrett who rapidly wrote down each word, "he is old. The young braves must carry on his work. He says he only fought the White Man, the Mexicans, for his land, his people. Now he has lost everything. But not his pride. If need be, he will fight again."

Barrett glanced up at the slumped, craggy, clay figure of the old warrior. His leathery face was infinitely sad. Geronimo spoke again. "He has," the major went on, "many times been wounded by the enemy—in his leg, knee, arm, head, eye, side, and back . . ." the major paused poignantly, "but never in his heart." Barrett stopped writing. He gazed into Geronimo's obsidian eyes.

"What treaty that the Whites have kept has the Red Man broken? Not one. What treaty that the White Man ever made with us have they kept? Not one. When I was a boy, the Apaches owned the world. The sun rose and set on our land. We sent ten thousand men to battle. Where are our warriors today? Who slew them? Where are our lands? Who owns them? What law have I broken? Is it wrong for me to love my own? Because my skin is red? Because I was born where my father lived? Because I would die for my people and my country?"

Geronimo paused. Ashamed, Barrett looked away. Then the old warrior spoke again, in soft Apache vowels, the major translating, "He says that you are taking me to a government place for my safety. Are you worried about my safety or your own? I am not fooled. Call it what you will, it is a prison and me a prisoner. You do your job for your people. I understand. But know this: I still have my job, too—for my people."

The major faltered as the Apache spoke on. He was moved as well. All the years he had cursed the man, and now as he sat next to him, he could see they were driven by the same desires, the same fears. A profound sadness engulfed him. He began translating again, his voice thick. "We are old enemies," Geronimo said, looking at the major almost with deep affection. "You are brave—I am old, cunning. Remember: Geronimo has escaped many times. It is eight hundred miles to your prison, twenty miles a day. We will see. . . ."

On the plains beyond the weather-beaten shacks were many buffalo. Their brown humps dotted the sparse grasslands like a living, moving guilt. Geronimo spoke again, softly, "Even if I am killed—or die—no matter. . . ." He looked off toward one massive buffalo who stood alone, as Geronimo had stood all his life. Its head was raised proudly and fiercely. Its huge horns were defiant, dangerous, poised, ready, capable of defending its life. "My Spirit will come back as a buffalo. Tell my people to look carefully when they hunt. They must never kill my Spirit. . . ."

The End